Fast Friends

Clint opened the door quietly, just a crack, just as the last of the bandidos was going by. If they had chosen to hit his room before Charlie's, there might have been a different outcome. He waited for the last man to go by, then swung the door open and stepped out into the hall, drawing his gun.

"Charlieeeeee!" he shouted just as the first bandido hit Charlie's door with a well-placed kick. There was an immediate shot, and the man went flying across the hall.

The remaining four men were unsure of which way to turn as Charlie came out into the hall, gun in hand. Clint immediately moved to his left, flattening himself against the wall as he fired . . .

THE GUNSMITH

302

THE FRIENDS OF WILD BILL HICKOK

J. R. ROBERTS

J

JOVE BOOKS, NEW YORK

THE BERKLEY PUBLISHING GROUP
Published by the Penguin Group
Penguin Group (USA) Inc.
375 Hudson Street, New York, New York 10014, USA
Penguin Group (Canada), 90 Eglinton Avenue East, Suite 700, Toronto, Ontario M4P 2Y3, Canada
(a division of Pearson Penguin Canada Inc.)
Penguin Books Ltd., 80 Strand, London WC2R 0RL, England
Penguin Group Ireland, 25 St. Stephen's Green, Dublin 2, Ireland (a division of Penguin Books Ltd.)
Penguin Group (Australia), 250 Camberwell Road, Camberwell, Victoria 3124, Australia
(a division of Pearson Australia Group Pty. Ltd.)
Penguin Books India Pvt. Ltd., 11 Community Centre, Panchsheel Park, New Delhi—110 017, India
Penguin Group (NZ), 67 Apollo Drive, Mairangi Bay, Auckland 1310, New Zealand
(a division of Pearson New Zealand Ltd.)
Penguin Books (South Africa) (Pty.) Ltd., 24 Sturdee Avenue, Rosebank, Johannesburg 2196,
South Africa

Penguin Books Ltd., Registered Offices: 80 Strand, London WC2R 0RL, England

This is a work of fiction. Names, characters, places, and incidents either are the product of the author's imagination or are used fictitiously, and any resemblance to actual persons, living or dead, business establishments, events, or locales is entirely coincidental.

THE FRIENDS OF WILD BILL HICKOK

A Jove Book / published by arrangement with the author

PRINTING HISTORY
Jove edition / February 2007

Copyright © 2007 by Robert J. Randisi.

ISBN: 978-0-515-14255-6

JOVE®
Jove Books are published by The Berkley Publishing Group,
a division of Penguin Group (USA) Inc.,
375 Hudson Street, New York, New York 10014.
JOVE is a registered trademark of Penguin Group (USA) Inc.
The "J" design is a trademark belonging to Penguin Group (USA) Inc.

PRINTED IN THE UNITED STATES OF AMERICA

10 9 8 7 6 5 4 3 2 1

ONE

MAGDALENA, NEW MEXICO

Clint Adams looked out his hotel window down at the main street of Magdalena. He counted them off. One . . . two . . . three . . . four . . . where was the other one? Oh, yeah, there he was . . . five.

From the bed behind him Eva's voice implored, "Come back to bed, *mi vida*. I am so lonely without you."

"In a minute."

"Those men will go away eventually," she told him.

"It's been three days," he said, turning to face her. "Three days since they arrived, three days since I've been out of this hotel."

The dark-haired, dark-eyed beauty sat up in bed and the sheet fell away from her. Her breasts were small but firm, with dark brown nipples, her body sleek and without blemish. He felt himself stirred immediately by the sight of her.

"They will grow tired," she said.

"They will not," he said. "Not those kind of men."

"What kind?"

"The kind hungry for a reputation," he told her. "They want to be known as the men who killed Clint Adams."

1

"Five against one?" she said, surprised. "Who would dare brag about such a thing?"

"Many men would brag that they had killed the Gunsmith," he said, "and leave out the fact that they were part of a mob."

Five hardly constituted a mob, but the general idea was there.

"Are you tired of being here with me?" she asked.

He was naked, and as she stared at him she saw that he was growing harder, rising more and more to the occasion with each passing moment.

"Never mind," she said, with a sly smile, "I can see that you are not."

He caught some movement outside the window and turned to see what it was. One of the men was shifting position. He was watching him when Eva's hand snaked around from behind him and grasped his semihard cock.

"If you will not come to me," she said in his ear, "I will come to you."

She pressed her body up against him, one hand stroking his penis, the other fondling his balls, brushing her hard nipples against his back.

"Eva . . ." he said.

"What is it?" she asked. "You do not like my hands?"

"I love your hand, *chica,* but—"

"Perhaps you would like my mouth better?"

Clint had met Eva in a cantina in town when he went there to eat and she had waited on him. She was tall and slender, with a wild mane of black hair, a full-lipped, wide mouth and black eyes. His cock got hard while she was serving him frijoles. Later that night, in his room, she served him something else.

Now, three days later, she wasn't tired of serving herself to him, and he wasn't tired of being served.

However, sometimes the fact that there were five men waiting out on the street to kill him—and that there was no back way out of the hotel—took the edge off his enjoyment of her.

But when she was like this—anxious, lustful, almost hungry for him—it was impossible to ignore her, especially when she had him in her hot, wet mouth like she did now.

She got between him and the window, stared up at him and said, "You can keep looking out the window. Don't pay any attention to me." She slid him into her mouth, began to suck him slowly, wetting him thoroughly, holding his testicles in one hand, gently massaging them.

"Eva, damn it—" he said, cupping her head and moving his hips in unison with her mouth. She released him from her mouth just so she could lick the length of him, tickle him in a sensitive spot just underneath his cock, and then swooped down to engulf him again.

Outside, the five men were moving around, maybe getting impatient after three days. One of them looked up at his window and he wondered what the man could see from down there.

Then he had a thought.

Down on the street Del Virtue and his gang waited for Clint Adams to come out of the hotel.

"This is crazy," Ben Horrigan said to Del. "It's been three days already. How do we even know he's still up there?"

"He's still up there," Virtue said. "Believe me."

"But how do we know?" Horrigan asked again.

"Because that horse of his is still in the livery stable," Virtue pointed out. "He's not goin' anywhere without that horse."

"It's just a damn horse," Horrigan said.

"You see that horse?" Steve Nash asked, joining them. "I sure as hell wouldn't leave an animal like that behind."

"Well," Horrigan said, "I still say we're wasting time. We don't even know for sure he's still up there."

Nash looked up at the window just then, took off his hat and ran his hand through his blond hair.

"You wanna know if he's still up there?" he asked Ben Horrigan. "Just take a look."

Horrigan and Del Virtue looked up at Clint Adams's hotel window, and Virtue smiled.

"What the hell is that?" Horrigan asked.

"You stupid fucker," Virtue said. "That's a woman's naked ass."

"Yep," Nash said, putting his hat back on. "He's up there, all right."

TWO

Just moments earlier Clint had reached down, slid his hands beneath Eva's arms and lifted her to her feet.

"You want to play games?" he asked. "We can play games."

"What are you doin'—"

He lifted her, put her naked ass right on the windowsill. The glass was cold against her back and she gasped, then gasped again as he slid his rigid cock into her and began to fuck her against the window.

"Ooh, oh, *dios mio*," she breathed, "people on the street, they will see—"

"Do you want me to stop?" he asked her.

"If you do," she said, "I will kill you!"

Clint braced his hands on the window frame and continued to fuck her, gliding in and out of her, slowly at first and then increasing the tempo. For a moment he had visions of the window giving way and both of them falling to the street, where he'd either be dead from a broken neck, or at the mercy of those five men without his gun. In the next moment he forgot all about that as Eva began to do something with her cunt, a trick she did that made it seem as if she were sucking him.

"Oh, *dios*," she said again, and then began babbling on in Spanish. "You are fucking me so good, hombre."

And giving those clowns on the street a show, he thought, and for a reason. But he'd shown them enough. He slid his hands beneath her ass, lifted her again and, without taking his cock from inside of her, walked back to the bed with her. Once there they fell onto the bed together, with him on top. When they landed on the mattress, it drove him even deeper inside of her, and she screamed. . . .

"Did you hear that?" Nash asked Virtue. "She's screamin'. He's givin' it to her good."

"Sure," Horrigan said. "He's havin' a good time up there while we're dyin' of boredom down here."

"He'll come out," Virtue said.

"What makes you so damn sure, all the time?" Horrigan demanded.

"He's got a damn reputation to protect," Virtue said. "He can't stay in there forever. The whole town's waitin' for him to come out. And when he does he can't run. He has to face us."

"One against five," Horrigan said. "Is he that stupid?"

"Maybe he's that good," Steve Nash said.

Virtue looked at him.

"Ain't nobody that good."

Clint was driving himself in and out of Eva so hard and fast that the bed was jumping off the floor with every stroke. She wrapped her legs around him and raked at his back with her nails as he drove her into a frenzy. What he was actually trying to do was finish her—and himself—so he could get on with the plan he'd just formed in his mind.

"*Aye, muchacho,*" she said, her voice raspy from the

heavy breathing she had been doing, "you are going to kill me."

If I don't kill myself first, he thought. Sweat started to drip from his chin onto her neck, filling the hollow there. He was almost ready to explode and wasn't going to be able to wait for her. But just at that moment, he felt her body tremble and then her release came and she bucked beneath him, crying out loud enough for the whole town to hear. A second later he exploded, bellowing like a bull. . . .

"You want me to do what?" she asked.

They were lying side by side in the bed, the perspiration drying on them as he told her his plan.

"I want you to—"

"No, I heard you," she said. "I just do not understand. Why do you want me to do that?"

"So I can get out of here."

"But . . . they are waiting."

"I'll go out the back."

"There is no back door."

"There are windows."

She sat up in bed and stared at him, incredulously.

"You, the great Gunsmith? *El Armero*? You would run?"

"To fight another day."

"But . . . why not fight today?" she asked. "I thought, these past few days, that you would soon walk out and kill those hombres."

Clint could see that he was going to have to explain the situation to Eva before she'd agree to help him. Facing five men in the street may have been a brave thing to do, but he was going to have to make her realize what a foolish thing it was to face those five men on their terms. When he faced them—and he would—he'd have to do it on his own terms.

It took him a good portion of the morning to get her to see things his way, and then she got dressed.

"I will be right back," she said.

"Don't leave the hotel," Clint said. "We don't want them to see you."

"I understand."

While she was gone, he walked to the window again—just to let his five friends see him one last time.

THREE

Del Virtue and his four partners had spotted Clint Adams in one of the saloons their first night in town. It was Virtue—the unofficial leader of the group—who recognized him.

"You know who that fella at the bar is?" he asked the others.

"Which fella?" Horrigan replied.

"That tall one at the end, talkin' to the barkeep."

"Why would I know who he is?"

"Because he's famous, you idiot."

"Famous for what?" Nash asked.

"Killin' people," Virtue said. "That there's Clint Adams."

Neal Jones leaned in and asked, "The Gunsmith? Is that who you're sayin' that feller is?"

"That's him."

"Son of a bitch," Nash said.

"He don't look like much," Mark Connors, the fourth partner, said.

"He ain't gonna be much when we get through with him," Virtue said. "He's gonna be dead."

• • •

Word had gotten back to Clint that there were five men waiting in the street to gun him down. The news came from the bartender at the Bonita Cantina, who had heard the talk. He then went to Clint's hotel to warn him.

"They plan to shoot you down in the street as soon as you step outside, senor," he'd told Clint.

"Thanks for the warning, Ignacio."

"What will you do?"

"Well," Clint said, "for one thing I won't be stepping out the front door anytime soon . . ."

Clint had to give the men credit. They had patience. He'd thought they'd get tired of waiting and go away eventually, but it didn't look like that was going to happen. For a while it looked like he was going to have to play it their way and step outside, take his chances on the street, but now he had a better idea. All he needed was for Eva to come back with—

There was a knock at his door. He'd gotten dressed and strapped on his gun, so he put his hand on the gun butt and walked to the door.

"Who is it?"

"It is me, Eva," she said. "I have the men—"

She stopped short when he opened the door. She was standing in the hall with three men.

"Okay, come on in," he told them all.

"Mister," one of the men said, "we're a little confused. This little lady told us to come with her, that the Gunsmith wanted to talk to us. Are you really the Gunsmith?"

"I am," he said, "and I do need some help, but only from one of you."

One man was short and too old. The second was young enough, but he was too heavy. The third man was the right age, wasn't as tall, but that probably wouldn't matter to the men on the street.

"Okay," he said to the other two, "you men can go.

Thanks for coming. Here." He gave them each a dollar. "Have a drink on me."

"Easiest drink I ever earned," one of them said, as they went out the door. The second man was too puzzled to speak.

The third man, who had asked Clint if he was the Gunsmith, stared at him.

"Am I gonna get a dollar, too?"

"Mister," Clint said, "you're going to get a heck of a lot more than a dollar."

The man looked pleased, but then surprised when Eva started taking off her dress.

"Don't just stand there," she said to him, "take off your clothes."

"Uh, what—" he started, but she hurried to undo his pants, pulling them down, followed by his underwear. The man was surprised, but that didn't stop his body from reacting.

Eva stood back and studied him.

"He is not as pretty as you," she said to Clint, "but he is a little . . . bigger."

"Hey," the man said, standing there with an erection. "What's goin' on? I don't go in for no funny stuff, ya know."

"Just stand there a minute," Clint told him. "You'll get ten dollars no matter what."

"Ten dollars? Just to—whoa—"

He stopped short when Eva took his cock in her hand and began to stroke it. It continued to grow impressively.

"What do you say, Eva?" Clint asked. "Do you approve?"

She ran her nail along the underside of the man's penis and he caught his breath. His cock began to twitch and she took her hand away, lest he finish too quickly.

"All right," she said, "I will do it, but only for you, *mi amor*."

"Mister," the other man said, "what's goin' on?"

"What's your name?"

"Sid."

"Sid," Clint asked, "how would you like to make twenty dollars and give Eva a poke?"

"I ain't gotta pay her?" Sid asked.

"No."

"And I get to keep the twenty?"

"Yes."

Suspicious, Sid asked, "What's the catch?"

"You're right to ask," Clint said. "There is a catch."

"I knew it!"

"Jesus Christ," Horrigan said. "They're at it again."

Nash, Virtue, Jones and Connors all looked up at Clint's window. There she was again, the naked woman with her ass pressed against the window.

"Why do they like doin' it against the window so much?" Jones asked.

"He's runnin' it in," Nash said. "Lettin' us know he's havin' a fine old time up there."

"Well," Virtue said, "we know one thing."

"What's that?" Horrigan asked.

"He's still up there."

Clint opened the window in the empty room, dropped his saddlebags to the ground, then considered dropping the rifle. Fearful that it might go off, he decided to keep it in one hand as he climbed out the window and stood there for a moment. Hoping he wouldn't break an ankle or twist a knee, he dropped to the ground. He landed with a grunt, but got quickly to his feet and checked himself. There were no injuries. He paused there a moment to see if anyone had heard him, but no one appeared. He grabbed his saddlebags and headed for the livery.

• • •

Up in the room Sid had his long, hard cock buried in Eva's hot pussy and was pumping away for all he was worth.

"Easy, easy," she told him, "'*pasito*, slowly. You must last."

"Oh, uh, sorry, miss."

He slowed down. Eva had to admit he had a nice long one, and it felt good going in and out of her. He was not as knowing as Clint Adams, but she'd had three days with Clint, and this man was different.

"Tell me, senor," she asked, "how long are you going to be in town?"

FOUR

Socorro, New Mexico

The ride from Magdalena to Socorro had been peaceful, uneventful. He wondered how long it had taken the five men to figure out the subterfuge he'd arranged for their entertainment, if they had figured it out yet—or at all. And if they had figured it out, he hoped they hadn't taken their anger out on Sid and Eva. And whenever they had figured it out, he wondered if they'd decided that they had missed their opportunity, or would they try to track him? In which case they'd catch up to him eventually, if they stuck with it. And hopefully, when they did, he'd be ready for them.

Socorro was bigger than Magdalena the way his middle finger was larger than his index finger. As he rode down the main street, he noticed two saloons and two hotels. Since he wasn't sure he was going to stay the night, he stopped at one of the saloons first. He chose it because the name above the door read, WILD BILL'S SALOON. That is, the name was above the door at one time, but at that moment two men were taking it down.

"What's going on?" he asked. "Are you open?"

"They're open," one of the men said. "They got a new owner."

"Is he changing the name?"

"Mister," the other man said, "we got hired to take the sign down, so I guess he is."

Clint decided to have a quick drink in Wild Bill's and then go across the street to the other saloon.

He went inside, found the place empty except for two men sitting in the back with their heads together, and a bartender looking bored behind the bar.

"Can I get a beer?" he asked, approaching the bar.

"Don't see why not," the bartender said.

The man drew a beer and set it on the bar. Clint looked around while he sipped at it. The usual saloon artwork was on the walls, nothing to indicate there was ever anything pertaining to Wild Bill Hickok. Maybe the "Wild Bill" of the sign was just a nickname of the owner. There was, after all, another Wild Bill other than Hickok, namely Wild Bill Longely.

"Looks like you're getting a name change," Clint said.

"New owner, new name."

"Was that the old owner's name?"

"No," the man said, still looking bored, "he called it that because he was best friends with Wild Bill Hickok."

"Is that a fact?"

Since James Butler Hickok had been Clint's best friend, it made him mad when anyone tried to trade on his late friend's name.

"Who would that be?" he asked.

"Fella sittin' in the back," the bartender said.

"There are two men back there."

"A buyer," the bartender said, "and a seller."

"What's the seller's name?"

"I don't know," the man said. "I work for the buyer. This is my first day."

"I can see you're all excited about it."

Clint left the bar with his beer and walked toward the back of the room, where the sale of the saloon seemed to have been completed. One man was rising while the other remained seated.

"Which of you is the seller?"

A dapper little man with long blond hair turned to face Clint and immediately a look of recognition crossed his face.

"Clint Adams?"

Clint studied the smaller man for a moment, searching his memory, and finally came up with a name.

"Charlie? Colorado Charlie Utter?"

"In the flesh."

Charlie Utter was the man who had buried Wild Bill Hickok. If anyone was a better friend to Hickok than Clint was, it was Utter.

"Well, horsewhip my ass," Utter said, grabbing Clint's hand and pumping it. "It's been years."

"What the hell are you doing here?" Clint asked. "Wild Bill's was yours?"

"*Was* is the right word," Utter said. "Now it belongs to a new owner, right here, who'll be glad to stand my friend and me to a beer."

The owner looked up and said, "Sure, Charlie. One last beer for ya."

"Thanks." Utter turned to Clint. "Come on, let's catch up."

They got two beers from the bartender, chose a table against the wall and sat together. Clint listened as Charlie told him the painful story of Bill Hickok's death and funeral.

"I went to Deadwood," Clint said, "but it was well after the fact. I'm glad you were there to, uh, take care of things."

"If I'd been there to back Bill up . . ." Charlie said, but let it fade out.

"There was no way you could have known, Charlie," Clint said. "Who knew what McCall had in mind when he entered the saloon?"

"Still," Charlie said, morosely, "if I'd been there . . ."

"How've you been doing since then, Charlie?"

"Not so good," the other man said. "Movin' from place to place. When I got here and opened my place, I thought I'd name it after Bill, you know? Like in his memory? That didn't really help me, though."

"You're too weighed down by guilt, Charlie," Clint said, "and it's been too many years for that."

"You're right," Charlie Utter said, "but there ain't much I can do about it, Clint, so why don't we just stop talkin' about it? What's been goin' on with you? I mean, all I ever heard are stories, you know? But I don't believe 'em all. Bill taught me that."

So Clint told him a bit about what he'd been doing, and finished up with the five men in Magdalena, who may or may not be on his trail.

FIVE

They went to a small cantina Charlie Utter knew had decent food and cold beer to finish catching up.

"If those five find their way here," Utter said over tacos and beer, "they'll have the two of us to deal with."

"I'd appreciate the backup, Charlie," Clint said. He knew better than to argue with the man. There was too much guilt in Charlie's past for him not to help, but the other thing was Clint knew that Charlie was an able man in a fight.

"Why're you selling your place, Charlie?"

Utter shrugged and said, "Just time to move on again, I guess."

"When were you thinking of leaving?"

"I was gonna head out tomorrow."

"Well, I'd be honored if you'd let me ride a while with you," Clint said. "It would give us some more time to talk."

"Long as we don't talk about Deadwood," Charlie said.

"We got lots of other stuff to talk about, Charlie," Clint assured him. "We can leave Deadwood in the past."

"Then I'd be honored to ride a ways with ya, Clint,"

"Good," Clint said. "Were you planning on an early start?"

"Yeah, they took my sign down and I didn't really wanna hang around here much longer. I was thinkin' first light . . . unless you wanted to spend some time here."

"I'm just passing through Socorro," Clint said. "I think I saw most of it while I was riding in."

"There ain't much more."

"Then first light suits me fine."

"I got me a room at the end of town," Charlie said. "It ain't much but you could sleep there if ya want."

"I can get a hotel room," Clint said. "That's not a problem."

"I forgot," Charlie said. "Bill always said ya went first class."

"I just like to have a mattress under me when I get off the trail," Clint said. "Figure I'll be sleeping on the ground again soon enough."

"One thing ya oughtta know, though, before you get on the trail with me," Charlie said.

"What's that?"

"I had me a run-in with a few fellas myself this past week," Utter said. "We might run into them out there."

"You back my play, Charlie," Clint said, "and I'll back yours."

"That sounds like a deal, Clint."

They left the cantina and Charlie said, "I still got some business ta take care of, Clint. How 'bout we meet later for a few more drinks before we turn in?"

"Sounds good to me. Meanwhile, I'll go and see about getting myself a hotel room. Any advice about which one to go to?"

"One's as bad as the other one," Charlie said, "but they both have mattresses."

"Right now," Clint said, "that's my only requirement."

The two agreed to meet later at the other saloon and parted company.

•   •   •

Clint got himself a room and realized not all mattresses were necessarily better than the ground. But since Charlie had said one hotel was as bad as the other, he kept the room. It was still better than sleeping in a small, cramped room with another man. When he had turned down Charlie's offer, he'd hoped the man would take his rejection without anger and felt lucky when he did.

Clint remembered back to when he had first heard of Hickok's death. He had crawled into a bottle for a long time. Later, when he sobered up, he realized two things. One, he'd felt guilty about not being able to keep Hickok from being killed by the coward Jack McCall. Two, there was no reason he should feel guilty, because he had not even been in Deadwood at the time.

But knowing how much guilt he had felt until coming to his senses, he still could not imagine the depth of Charlie Utter's guilt. After all, Utter *had* been in Deadwood at the time, just not in that particular saloon.

For more than ten years, then, Utter had been haunted by that guilt no matter where he went or what he did. He wondered, in all that time, if Utter had talked to anybody. But who do you talk to when it's your best friend—the man you talked to about all your problems—who is dead?

Maybe riding together for a while would give Charlie somebody to talk to, and maybe he could talk away some of that guilt. At least, that was what Clint hoped he could offer the man. After all, they had something in common. They had both been friends of Wild Bill Hickok.

SIX

Clint arrived at the second saloon in town and saw that Charlie wasn't there yet. He went to the bar, got himself a beer from a bartender who was a lot friendlier than the other one had been that afternoon, and settled in to wait.

Business was very good, he saw, and wondered if this might have been another reason Charlie had sold out. Maybe his competition had driven him out of business. There wasn't much difference between the places physically that he could see, but he had never seen Charlie's place in action. This one had a couple of table games going, and some pretty Mexican gals working the floor.

"Pretty solid business," Clint said to the bartender, who was a gringo.

"We do okay."

"Better than the place across the street?"

"That one just changed hands today," the man said. "If the new owner knows what he's doin' he might give us some competition."

"No competition from the old owner?"

The bartender, a man in his mid-forties with a solid stomach, had the quick hands of a man who had been doing his job for many years.

23

"His heart wasn't really into runnin' the place," the man said. "Sellin' it was probably the best thing for him."

"You know him well?"

"Just to talk to," the bartender said. "Came to town 'bout a year ago, bought the place, gave it a new name . . ." He shrugged. "He just never did nothin' with it. You know him?"

"I did, years ago," Clint said. "Saw him today for the first time in a while."

"Always claimed to be friends with Hickok," the barman said. "That was why he named the place Wild Bill's. Any of that talk true?"

"All of it," Clint said. "He was Wild Bill Hickok's best friend."

"Really?" The man looked surprised.

"You never believed him?"

"Well . . . lots of people make up stories to make themselves important, ya know?"

"Well, Charlie didn't have to make that one up," Clint said.

"Whataya know about that? Did you know Hickok, too?"

"I had that honor."

Suddenly, the fortyish bartender was like a young boy.

"Jeez, that musta been great, bein' friends with a legend."

"Yeah," Clint said, "it was pretty great."

"Hey, here comes your friend now."

"Get him a beer, will you?"

"Sure thing."

Charlie looked around, spotted Clint and came over to join him. By the time he did, the bartender was back with his beer.

"Here ya go, Mr. Utter."

Charlie took the beer and frowned at Clint as the bartender was called away to the other end of the bar.

"Mr. Utter?" Charlie said. "He ain't called me mister since the day I got here."

"Guess he knows better now," Clint said.

"What'd you tell him?"

"Just that you were Bill's best friend."

Charlie looked pained.

"Guess I used ta shoot my mouth off when I got drunk," he said. "Nobody around here believed me, anyway."

"Well, they will now," Clint said. "The bartender will spread the word."

"Did you tell him who you was?"

"No," Clint said, "just that I was friends with Bill, too."

"Bill used ta talk about you a lot," Charlie said. "He claimed you was the best hand with a gun he ever saw."

"There's better," Clint said, "including Bill."

"Not accordin' ta him," Charlie said. "I never heard him talk about nobody like he talked about you."

"That's real nice of you to say, Charlie."

"It's true."

Clint lifted his beer mug and said, "To Wild Bill Hickok."

"To Bill," Charlie said.

They drank to their friend and then Charlie took a look around the place.

"This place don't have a name," he said.

Clint had wondered about that on the way in.

"I thought if I bought the place across the street and gave it a name, I might do okay, but it takes more than that," he went on. "Ya gotta care, ya know? I just stopped carin' a long time ago."

"I understand," Clint said. "I had a hard time myself after I heard of Bill's death. Spent some time drinking heavily."

"But you got over it."

"I stopped drinking," Clint said. "I don't know that I

ever got over it. How do you get over losing a friend, especially that way."

"Goddamn coward!" Charlie swore. "And then they let him loose. Thank God they tried him legal in Yankton and hanged the bastard."

Clint agreed. If Jack McCall had gone scot-free, he shuddered to think what that would have done to Charlie Utter.

"Charlie, let's go get a steak."

"That sounds good," Utter said. He put his beer on the bar, unfinished, which Clint found encouraging.

They shared a steak and then went their separate ways to meet again at first light at the livery stable.

Clint went to his room to work on his guns. He didn't know where Charlie Utter went, but he hoped it was to bed.

SEVEN

Where there was once a sign that read WILD BILL'S SA-
LOON, there was now one that read THE RED GARTER. As
Charlie Utter entered and looked around, he saw paintings
on the wall of women of all sizes and shapes, with one
thing in common—they all wore red garters, and nothing
else. He looked around further and saw that the place was
more crowded than it had ever been as Wild Bill's.

"Why didn't I think of that?" he muttered to himself.

"Hello, Charlie."

He turned and saw Ed Conlon, the man who had bought
the place, standing next to him. He was wearing a black
gambler's suit and smoking a big, fat cigar.

"Not bad, eh?" Conlon asked.

"I knew you'd make a go of it, Ed," Utter said. "I'm
here for the rest of my money. I'm gonna be headin' out tomorrow morning."

"Leavin' us so soon?"

"Sooner the better."

"All right," Conlon said. "Come on back to your—I
mean, my office, and I'll give you the rest."

Charlie followed Conlon through the crowded saloon
and no one so much as said hello to him. The thing he had

27

always liked about Bill was that he could talk to him. Since Hickok's death Charlie had no one to talk to. He just wasn't the type to make friends. That was why it had been such a bad idea for him to open a saloon.

In the office Conlon went around what used to be Charlie's desk and opened a drawer. He took out a long brown envelope and tossed it onto the desktop.

"Count it," he suggested. "It's all there."

"I trust you, Ed," Charlie said, picking up the envelope and feeling its thickness. "Besides, if it ain't I'll just come back and put a bullet in ya."

Conlon stared at Utter and fidgeted uncomfortably, not knowing whether or not the man was serious.

"I'm kiddin' ya, Ed."

"Oh."

"Thanks for this," Utter said, holding up the envelope and then tucking it away inside his shirt. "I'll be on my way."

"You know, Charlie," Conlon said, before Charlie could reach the door, "you could have gotten more. Why did you sell so cheap?"

"It's enough for me," Utter said, patting the envelope through his shirt. "I just wanted to sell and be on my way."

"Have a beer on the way out," Conlon said. "Tell the bartender you got one more free one coming."

"Maybe I'll do that, Ed," Utter said. "Thanks."

As Charlie came out of the office, touching his chest where his money was, one man nudged another man, the two of them seated at the same table.

"I told you," he said. "He came back for the rest of his money."

The other man laughed and said, "You mean the rest of our money."

The two men laughed together.

• • •

Charlie decided to skip the last free beer in The Red Garter and just go to his room. It would be his last night there, and he couldn't wait to get it over with. He never wanted to see that room again after tomorrow.

After Clint had finished cleaning his rifle and modified Colt, he got bored. It was too early to go to sleep, so he strapped on his holster and went back out. He decided to go and see what kind of business Charlie's old place was doing.

He was walking toward the saloon when he saw Charlie Utter come walking out. He was about to call out to him when the batwing doors opened again and two men came out. They were nudging each other, and they both drew their guns. They fell in behind Charlie, who was oblivious to their presence.

Fortunately, Clint was not.

"Hold it right there, you two!"

Charlie Utter turned at the sound of Clint Adams's voice, saw the two men behind him as they turned on Clint with their guns. They already had their guns out, and his was holstered. Utter could see Clint clearly in the moonlight, but he never saw him draw his gun; it was as if it just appeared in his hand.

Before the two men could fire, Clint Adams squeezed off two shots. The two men staggered, dropped their guns, and fell, one facedown, and the other on his back.

Charlie never had a chance to get his own gun out.

"You all right?" Clint asked Utter, as they converged over the two dead men.

"I'm fine," Utter said, still in shock. "Bill was right about you."

"What?" Clint leaned over and checked both men to be sure they were dead. Then he ejected the two spent shells from his gun, reloaded and holstered it.

"When Bill said you was the fastest he'd ever seen," Utter went on, "he was right. I-I never saw you draw."

"Charlie, what were you doing in there?"

"Gettin' the rest of my money."

"Well, they must have known that," Clint said. "They were going to kill you and take it from you."

"They woulda been disappointed," Utter said.

"Why's that?"

"I sold cheap."

Clint looked around. Some men had come out of each of the saloons and were watching them. Someone had probably gone for the sheriff already.

"We're going to have to wait for the sheriff," he said to Utter.

"Don't worry," Charlie said. "I know 'im. Clint . . . you saved my life."

"Don't mention it."

"How do I pay you back?"

"Like I said, Charlie," Clint replied, "don't mention it."

EIGHT

The sheriff's name was Roxton, and the fact that he knew Charlie Utter didn't seem to work in their favor very much. He marched them to his office and once there demanded their guns.

"He can't give you his gun, Sheriff," Utter said, before Clint could respond for himself.

"Why the hell not?"

"You know who he is," Utter went on. "He told you right out there on the street. Clint Adams. The Gunsmith. You take his gun away from him, he's a dead man." Charlie looked at Clint. "Ain't that the way it is? That's the way it used to be with Bill."

"That's pretty much it," Clint said.

Roxton, an unimpressive-looking man in his fifties, glared at Utter, then looked at Clint.

"You won't give me your gun?"

"I'm going to my room, Sheriff, and then we're leaving in the morning," Clint said. "No, I won't give you my gun."

"You gonna make me take it from you?"

Clint smiled.

"I'm going to make you try."

Suddenly, he changed his tactic. He looked at Utter.

"Come on, Charlie," he said. "You and me is friends. Can't you get him to gimme his gun?"

"Oh, so now we're friends?" Utter asked, with a short laugh. "I wouldn't get him ta give you his gun even if I could. And I'll tell ya somethin' else. I ain't givin' ya mine, either."

"Yer just makin' my job harder, Charlie."

"Well, we're gonna make it a lot easier for ya when we leave tomorrow," Charlie said, "and I don't aim ta get killed between now and mornin'. Now, we tol' ya what happened on the street. Go talk to the witnesses if you don't believe us."

"You know as well as I do that everybody out there was drunk, and that nobody saw nothin'. They didn't even come out of the saloons till they heard the shots."

"Sheriff," Clint said, "you're either going to try to take my gun or I'm going back to my hotel."

Roxton glared at both of them this time, then cursed and said, "Ah, get outta my office—and get outta town tomorrow at sunup."

"We was gettin' out anyway, ya stupid—"

"Let's go, Charlie," Clint said, cutting Utter off. "Let's not make the man's job harder still."

Clint directed Utter out of the sheriff's office before he forced the lawman to do something they'd all regret.

"Guess I was pretty stupid," Charlie said as they approached the hotel. Clint had told Charlie to get a room, just in case somebody else wanted to steal his money.

"When?" Clint asked. "On the street or in the sheriff's office?"

"Both, I guess," Utter said. "I was gonna let those two sneak up on me. They probably woulda killed me."

"I don't think there's any probably about it, Charlie," Clint said. "They were going to kill you and take your money. Who else knows you got all that money on you?"

"Well, I guess everybody who was in that saloon tonight."

"Great."

"And I'm sorry I butted in with the sheriff," Utter said. "I'm sure you coulda tol' him yerself that you wasn't givin' up your gun."

"Yes. I could have."

"I used ta do those things for Bill, ya know? The little things he couldn't be bothered ta do? Back then, in Deadwood, we was supposed to be prospectin', ya know? But all he wanted ta do was play poker."

"Well, you don't have to do the little things for me, Charlie," Clint said. "I can do them myself."

"Yeah, I know," Utter said.

They entered the lobby and had to rouse the clerk from a back room in order to get Charlie a place to sleep for the night. Once they had a key, the clerk didn't even bother going back to the room behind the curtain. He just put his head down on the desk and went back to sleep.

When they got upstairs, they found that Charlie's room was right across from Clint's.

"You can collect the rest of your things from your room tomorrow," Clint said. "For tonight let's just keep you alive."

"I'm much obliged, Clint," Charlie said. "I don't know if I've said it enough times."

"You said it plenty, Charlie," Clint said. "Just go inside and get some sleep."

"Right."

Charlie unlocked the door and went in, but before the door closed Clint called out, "And keep your gun handy."

"Right on the bedpost, where Bill used ta keep his when he was sleepin'," Charlie promised.

And where Clint kept his whenever he was in a hotel room.

He used his key to unlock his own door and went inside. Maybe Charlie used to do all the little things for Bill

Hickok back in the day, but the man sure did need some-body to look after *him* now. Clint wasn't after the job, but maybe he could wake Charlie up a bit, make him care about his life more, and then he could do all those things for himself.

NINE

The night went by uneventfully and in the morning it was Charlie who banged on Clint's door to wake him up.

"I'm up," Clint said, opening the door.

"Used ta have to wake Bill up every day," Charlie said. "I know, I know, you ain't Bill. I gotta stop doin' that."

Clint was glad he hadn't had to tell Charlie that himself. He was starting to get tired of hearing about the things he did for Bill, but he didn't want to hurt Charlie's feelings by telling him to shut up about it.

"Just give me a second."

Clint backed into the room, picked up his rifle and saddlebag and said, "Now let's go and get your stuff, and then we can get to the livery. You do have a horse, don't you?"

"Yeah, I got a horse. I ain't used him much, lately," Charlie admitted, "but I got one."

They went down to the lobby and when Clint tried to pay for the room, Charlie stopped him and took out his own money.

"I pay my own way," he said as they left the hotel, which was okay with Clint.

• • •

Clint saw that he'd been right about not wanting to share Charlie's place the night before. It turned out to be a pretty run-down shack on the edge of town that wasn't much bigger than an outhouse.

"Why didn't you just stay in the saloon?" Clint asked him.

"I wanted to get away from there when I wasn't workin'," Charlie said. "Didn't want nobody findin' me so easy if there was trouble."

As Charlie collected his belongings—what there was of them—Clint wondered how the man had even managed to run the saloon for a year with that attitude.

"Okay, the livery next."

When they got to the livery and Clint saw Charlie's horse, he felt better. She was a pretty sturdy-looking mare who would carry him a long way. They each saddled their animals and Charlie couldn't get over what a beautiful animal Eclipse was.

"I ain't never seen a horse this fine," Charlie said.

Clint couldn't remember if Charlie Utter had ever seen Duke, the gelding he'd had before Eclipse.

They walked their horses outside and got mounted.

"We need some supplies?" Charlie asked.

"I got some coffee and hardtack," Clint said. "That's about all I need when I'm traveling, unless I actually plan on being on the trail a lot longer."

"Bill used ta—never mind."

They rode out of Socorro without another word between them, and it stayed like that for about fifteen minutes before Charlie couldn't stand it and started talking.

He talked nonstop for the next three hours. . . .

"I guess I better shut up for a while," he said, finally.

"With all the talking you've done, Charlie," Clint said,

"you never once said where you were going—or where you were thinking of going."

They had stopped to rest the horses and get some water at a nearby water hole. Now they were sitting on a couple of rocks for a few moments more before continuing.

"I ain't never been to ol' Mexico," Charlie said. "I think maybe it's time I had a look."

"It's a beautiful place," Clint said. "Most of it, anyway."

"They say you can go to the ocean," Charlie said. "You seen the ocean, Clint?"

"I have."

"And the women," the other man went on. "I heard Mexican gals is the most beautiful in the world."

"If you like black-haired, black-eyed gals with smooth skin, I guess they are," Clint said.

"Then that's what I'm gonna do," Charlie said. "I'm goin' ta ol' Mexico."

"Good for you."

"You wanna come with me?" Charlie asked.

"I don't know, Charl—"

"When's the last time you was there?"

"It's been a while."

"Then why don' you come?" Charlie asked. "Unless you got somethin' else ta do."

Clint had nothing pressing to do, but he wasn't sure he wanted to go to Mexico with Charlie Utter. He'd been hoping to talk some sense into the man in a day or two, but damned if Utter ever shut up long enough for Clint to get a word in.

"I tell you what I can do," Clint said. "I can ride to the border with you, and then make up my mind."

"That sounds good to me," Charlie said. "We got to go to Texas ta do this?"

"We can go to El Paso," Clint said. "It's an easy crossing there."

"Well, there ya go," Charlie Utter said. "I ain't never been El Paso way, neither."

"Then I guess we'd better get a move on," Clint said. "When you're going to experience new things, it's best to just get to it."

TEN

When they camped that night, Clint made a pot of coffee and shared his hardtack with Charlie.

"I forgot to ask you," Clint said, as they sat across the fire from each other. "Those two who tried to rob you, were they the ones you had trouble with before?"

"No," Utter said. "I never saw those two before. I had some trouble with a couple of saddle tramps in my place, but as far as I know they left town."

"Well," Clint said, "just to be on the safe side we'd better stand watch. I've still got five guns out who may be looking for me and you've got two."

"No problem," Charlie said. "I'll take first watch and wake you in four hours."

"Okay."

Charlie poured himself some more coffee and said, "You make pretty good trail coffee."

"It's my specialty," Clint said. "I like it black and strong."

"It's strong, all right," Colorado Charlie said. "I could clean my gun with this."

"Go ahead," Clint said. "It's good for a lot of things, but mostly for warming the insides."

Not that they needed it. It was a mild night, no chill in the air at all, which was fine with Clint. It was bad enough sleeping on the ground, but when the ground was cold that was even worse.

Clint made a bed for himself, using his saddle and his bedroll, and settled into it. He turned on his left side so he wouldn't be lying on his gun. At no time, even in his sleep, would he turn onto his right side. It was that ingrained in him that it wouldn't happen—ever.

Charlie was sitting with his back to Clint, who thought that the slump of Utter's shoulders was possibly the saddest thing he had ever seen.

When Utter shook him he came immediately awake.

"Everything okay?" he asked.

"Fine," Utter said. "Real quiet. I drank all the coffee, figured you'd wanna make another pot yerself."

"That's good," Clint said, rolling out of his bedroll and getting quickly to his feet.

"Want me to stay awake while you wake up a little?" Charlie offered.

"That's okay, Charlie," Clint said. "I'm awake."

Charlie opened his mouth to say something, then caught himself. He was probably going to say how Hickok woke like that. So instead he went and prepared a place for himself to sleep.

"I'll wake you at first light," Clint said.

"I'll be ready," Charlie promised, rolling himself up in his blanket. In seconds, Clint heard snoring.

Charlie had taken the empty coffeepot off the fire and it was cold. There was no longer the smell of coffee in the air, as there had been when he'd lain down to go to sleep. But there was something else . . .

He set the coffeepot down, stood and walked to the edge of the circle of light thrown by the fire. He did it as if standing there would enable him to smell the air better. And maybe it worked.

"Bacon," he said to himself, sniffing the air. . . .

Del Virtue accepted the plate of bacon and beans Steve Nash handed him and began eating.

"That ain't a good idea," Ben Horrigan said.

"Don't eat any, then. More for me."

"I mean, they're liable to smell it."

"Who?"

"Adams and the other fella with him."

"They told us in Socorro that the other fella's name was Charlie Utter," Virtue said.

"Colorado Charlie Utter," Nash said, handing a plate to Horrigan, who took it, good idea or not.

"He was a friend of Wild Bill Hickok's," Neal Jones said from across the fire. "Story goes he buried Hickok."

"So what does that get him?" Nash asked. "Special treatment? He'll be just as dead as Adams when we catch up to them."

"I don't even know why we're doin' this," Horrigan said. "This is a wild goose chase."

"Clint Adams, that's why," Nash said.

The fifth man, Mark Connors, shook his head and said, "I gotta agree with Ben. We could be makin' some money, now. We passed up a few banks that looked like cracker boxes to me."

"Why don't you and Ben go on back and make some withdrawals then?" Virtue asked. "Steve and Neal and I will keep after Adams. By the time you meet up with us, we'll have the rep as bein' the Gunsmith's killers."

Nash sat down with his own plate of food.

"You know," Horrigan said, "with the smell of bacon and beans in camp we'd never smell it if they was cooking somewhere up ahead of us."

"The wind's blowin' away from us, anyway," Virtue said.

"Which means they can smell us, but we can't smell them," Horrigan pointed out.

"Good," Virtue said, "it'll let Adams know we're comin'. Coward climbed out a window to get away from us. What kind of a legend does that?"

The kind, Horrigan thought, who was smart enough not to face five men in the street, but he kept the comment to himself.

ELEVEN

When Clint shook Charlie Utter awake in the morning, the man did not wake well.

"Been a long time since I slept on the ground," he said, standing and stretching his back.

"Have some coffee and let's get moving," Clint said. "We've got some company."

"Where?" Charlie asked, accepting a cup of coffee.

"Don't know, behind us somewhere," Clint said. "I could smell bacon and beans last night when you woke me."

Charlie frowned as he sipped some scalding coffee.

"I didn't smell nothin'," he said.

"You need to get your trail senses back," Clint said. "It won't take long. You've still got them, they've just been . . . ignored for so long."

"I feel like a fool," Charlie said. "That ain't somethin' I woulda missed in the old days."

"Like I said Charlie," Clint repeated, "it'll all come back to you, soon enough."

Virtue and his gang broke camp and saddled their horses. He took an opportunity to pull Horrigan aside and talk to him.

"So, you stayin' or goin'?"

"Goin' where, Del?"

"You keep talkin' about leavin'. Goin' to rob a bank or somethin'," Virtue said. "I wanna know if you're goin'."

"Aw, I'm not goin' anywhere, Del," Horrigan said. "You know me, I'm just a talker."

"Well, try talkin' a little less, Ben," Virtue said. "I don't want the others catchin' it from you. Got it?"

"I got it, Del."

"Good," Virtue said, "then get mounted."

Once they were all mounted, Steve Nash asked, "Which way are we headed, Del?"

Virtue looked at Neal Jones, who was their tracker.

"This way," Jones said. "Although if they keep goin' in this direction, they're gonna take us to El Paso, or . . ."

"Or what?" Virtue asked.

"Across the border, Del," Nash said. "Are we gonna chase Adams in Mexico?"

"Mexico," Virtue said. "Hell, and back . . ."

Clint stamped out the fire as he and Charlie Utter broke camp. He turned and caught Charlie staring off into the distance behind them.

"You think it's your five?" Charlie asked.

Clint went over and stood next to the smaller man.

"I hope it's only five," he said, "and that they haven't picked up a few more along the way."

"It's not like there's a price on your head," Charlie said.

"You've been through this with Bill many times," Clint reminded him. He was also giving Charlie leave to go ahead and talk about it.

"I know it," he said. "What is it about men like you and Bill that makes men . . ."

"Want to shoot us in the back?"

"They're not all Jack McCall."

"No," Clint said, "some of them come right at you, but they do it with three or four friends. Like that's somehow better than an out and out bushwhacking."

"If they trail us all the way to El Paso, there's law there," Charlie said. "And then once we're in Mexico . . ."

"These kind of men won't be stopped by the border, Charlie," Clint said. "If they don't try to ambush us between here and El Paso, they'll just follow us into Mexico—that is, if I go into Mexico. In fact, it might be better for you if we split up now."

Charlie looked at him.

"And what if it's me they're after?" Charlie asked.

"They might not follow you into Mexico," Clint said. "Unless you've aggrieved them so badly that they will?"

"I won't know if I've aggrieved them until we see who they are," Charlie said. "Why don't we stay together and watch each other's backs until we do see them?"

"Suits me," Clint said. "If it's those same five from Magdalena, I could use the help."

As they mounted up, Charlie said, "I don't think Bill woulda done what you did. I mean, goin' out that window like you did."

"Meaning?"

"Meaning he had more of an ego than you," Charlie said. "I woulda said, 'Bill, here's the smart thing to do,' and he woulda said, 'Charlie, how could I look at my face in a mirror if I did that?' And I'd say, 'At least you'd be alive to look in the mirror, Bill.' You know what he'd say to me?"

"That if he was alive after running like that he wouldn't want to look in the mirror," Clint said.

"That's exactly right."

"Charlie," Clint said, "I look at myself in the mirror just fine."

"I didn't mean—"

"Sometimes it's killing men that makes me not want to look in the mirror."

He urged Eclipse forward before Charlie could comment on that.

TWELVE

By the time they reached El Paso, Charlie Utter had some of his trail senses back. They made cold camp a few times, munching on hardtack but not making coffee so they could sniff the air for telltale signs of someone else's camp. Sure enough, Charlie picked up the scent of bacon.

One night out from El Paso they made coffee and sat around the fire, talking.

"Whoever that is behind us is gonna end up in El Paso," Charlie Utter opined.

"They may just be heading in the same direction we are," Clint said. "If they wanted to catch us, they should have been able to."

"Maybe they did," Charlie said. "Maybe they got a look, saw two of us and didn't like the odds. Cowards who like five-to-one odds would balk at five-to-two, I think."

"You're probably right about that, Charlie. But they're not going to get better odds in El Paso."

"Maybe they'll just wait and see if we go into ol' Mexico," Charlie said. "Their odds would be a lot better there, with no law to worry about once we cross."

"Well, all this talk is fine, my friend," Clint said, "but we'll just have to wait and see."

They set their watches the same way—Charlie first, Clint second—and Clint turned in.

"We're a day and a half out of El Paso," Horrigan complained. "When are we gonna make our move?"

"We're gonna wait," Virtue said. "I decided to see what happens when we get to El Paso."

"Why?" Horrigan asked. "You sent Steve ahead to scout it out. There's only two of them."

"Because I make the decisions, Ben, remember?" Virtue asked. "And all you do is talk. Remember you told me that?"

"Yeah, but—"

"I'll tell you what I want you to do from now on, Ben," Virtue said, cutting him off.

"What?" Horrigan frowned suspiciously.

"I want you to stop talkin', stop thinkin'," Virtue said, "and just do what you're told. Can you do that?"

"Yeah, but—"

"Because if you can't do that," Virtue said, "you're no use to me."

The two men stared at each other for a few moments, then Horrigan looked away.

"Tell Steve to come over here," Virtue told Horrigan.

The man nodded and went to run his errand. Steve Nash appeared next to Virtue a few moments later.

"What'd you do to Ben?" he asked. "He wouldn't even talk, just jerked his thumb at me."

"Never mind," Virtue said. "I want you to ride ahead again and follow them into El Paso. See where they go."

"Where do you expect them to go?"

"I dunno," Virtue said. "A hotel, the sheriff's office? A saloon? I just wanna know where to find them when we get to town."

Nash shrugged.

"Okay," he said. "I'll see where they go and then I'll wait for you at the smallest cantina in town."

"That's a good idea," Virtue said. "You got any idea who the law is in El Paso?"

"Naw," Nash said. "Used ta be Dallas Stoudenmire, but he's been dead a while."

"Okay," Virtue said. "You get goin' at first light, we'll probably see you later in the day."

"Sure thing, Del."

"And get me another plate, will ya? I'm still hungry."

"Comin' up."

When it was Clint's watch, he made a full pot of coffee for himself. As he sat at the fire drinking it—careful not to look into the flames—he gave some thought to Charlie Utter's progress over the past few days. He seemed to be getting back to himself. He was sitting his horse better, not complaining so much about sleeping on the ground, and he was more aware of his surroundings. He was more like the man who used to back Hickok and then shepherd him around when his eyesight started going and he was drinking a bit too much.

Clint knew that Wild Bill Hickok's last days in Deadwood were not happy ones. He'd stopped wearing a badge, still unable to get over the fact that he'd shot one of his own deputies in Abilene because of bad eyesight. Maybe having a friend like Charlie Utter made things a little better for him. At least, he hoped so.

Of course, it couldn't have been very easy for Charlie to deal with an ornery, often drunk Hickok. Clint knew how stubborn Bill could be when he was right-minded. Drunk, he was probably impossible.

He turned and looked over at the sleeping form of Colorado Charlie Utter. The man must have had the patience of a saint back then.

Clint poured himself another cup of coffee. Now he thought about whoever it was who was riding behind them, probably about a half day back. If it was the five men from

Magdalena, he was definitely going to need Charlie's help to fend them off. If that happened, and they came out of it alive, he was going to feel obligated to accompany the man into Mexico, which Charlie seemed intent on seeing. Well, Clint had been to worse places than Mexico. It was true that the women were beautiful, and that if you rode long enough and far enough you'd get to see the ocean.

Yeah, he'd spent days doing much worse.

THIRTEEN

El Paso was the way Clint had left it the last time he was
there, except for one thing. Dallas Stoudenmire had gone
and gotten himself killed. Clint didn't know who the law in
El Paso was now, but it didn't matter. He didn't intend for
them to be in town long enough to get into trouble.

"A meal and a mattress for one night," was what he told
Charlie Utter as they rode in.

"And a drink," Charlie added.

"A quick one," Clint agreed.

"What're you gonna do come mornin'?" Charlie asked.
"You comin' ta Mexico?

"I guess I'll decide that tonight, Charlie," Clint replied.
"First let's get a steak into our bellies."

"I hope you mean one each," Charlie quipped.

That was something else Clint had noticed about Charlie, he seemed to have gotten his sense of humor back.

They took their horses to a livery stable first, made sure
they were well taken care of and then took their rifles and
saddlebags over to the nearest hotel. On the way they
passed a bridge that would take them across to Ciudad
Juarez, El Paso's sister city in Mexico.

They stopped at the first hotel they came to, one that had

a cantina attached. It was an adobe building, all one floor, the rooms stretched out behind the cantina. They stopped at the bar and got two beers and two rooms at the same time.

Over the beers Clint asked the bartender, "Can we get a couple of steaks, or is it all Mexican food?"

"Steaks are our specialty," the bartender said. "You want Mexican food, go across the border."

"Fine, then can we get a couple of steak dinners going while we put our gear in our rooms?"

"Sure."

"Friendly guy," Charlie said as they walked down the hall to their rooms. As they passed other closed doors, they heard a woman screaming and a man bellowing.

"That reminds . . ." Charlie commented, but he left the rest unsaid.

Clint went back to talking about the bartender.

"If he hates Mexican food so much, why doesn't he go live somewhere else?" he wondered.

"I just hope the steaks are good."

They found their rooms, seven and nine with one between them. The rooms did not run odd numbers on one side and even on the other, but simply went in a row.

They each opened their doors just long enough to toss their saddlebags on the bed. They decided to keep their rifles with them. As they walked back, they could still hear the man and woman going at it.

"Sounds like he's gettin' his money's worth," Charlie said.

"Sounds like it."

"Might try some of that myself, later."

Clint didn't respond.

"You like whores, Clint?"

"A whore's fine," Clint said, "as long as I don't have to pay."

"Yeah, well, I ain't the ladies man you are. I ain't got the patience, anyway. I'd rather just pay a woman and not have to talk to her."

"To each his own," Clint said.

When they got back to the cantina, the bartender waved them to a table, and a black-haired Mexican girl came out of the back carrying two steaming plates. In front of each of them she placed a huge slab of beef, refried beans and some tortillas.

"Cerveza?" she asked them.

"*Sí*," Clint said, "*dos* cervezas."

"*Sí*, senor."

"You talk Mex?" Charlie asked.

"You just heard it all."

"She was a pretty gal," Charlie said. "I wonder if she whores, too."

"You can ask her," Clint said, then added, "after we eat."

"Sure, Clint, sure."

The girl came back with two beers and set them down with a smile. She couldn't have been more than eighteen and she wore a low-cut peasant blouse that showed where her nipples were. She had small breasts, but large nipples, which Charlie couldn't take his eyes off of.

"If you need anything else, senors, my name is Carmen."

"*Gracias,* Carmen," Clint said.

The steaks were perfect, running with red, which they soaked up with the tortillas. The bartender, a big gringo in his thirties with thick forearms, yelled at the girl once or twice, calling her stupid when he told her to do something.

"That fella shouldn't treat that girl that way," Charlie said.

"She probably works for him."

"Still, it seems like he don't like anything Mex, food or girls."

"Forget it, Charlie," Clint said. "We're not here to start any trouble or play the hero. She's not a damsel in distress."

"Huh?"

"Just eat."

"Seems to me he's the one startin' trouble, talkin' to her like that," Charlie muttered.

"Charlie," Clint said, warningly, "if you're suddenly in love with Carmen, just take her to your room and have her, but don't start anything here. How do we know what their relationship is like? Maybe they're even married."

"Married? Him and her?" Charlie looked appalled. "That couldn't be—could it?"

"You never know, Charlie," Clint said. "You just never know."

Steve Nash followed Clint Adams and Charlie Utter into El Paso, confident that they didn't know they had a tail. He was good only at a few things, he admitted, and following people was one of them.

Once in town, he was able to dismount, tie his horse off and stay with them on foot. They weren't riding through town very fast. He watched them go to the livery, and then into the cantina that had rooms in the back. He peered in the window long enough to determine that they had taken some rooms, and then saw them sit down to some food. His stomach growled, and then something else twitched when he saw the Mexican waitress bring them some food.

He went back to his horse, satisfied that he knew where they were so he could tell Del Virtue. But Virtue and the others wouldn't be in town for some time. So before going to look for the smallest cantina in town, Nash decided to go and find the local cathouse.

It wasn't until much later that he discovered that the very cantina Clint and Charlie Utter had gone into, where they had taken rooms and gotten a couple of steak dinners, was also the smallest cantina in town.

FOURTEEN

Charlie wanted to go out and walk around El Paso after they ate. Clint didn't want to. He'd seen El Paso before. But he couldn't let Charlie go alone, so he accompanied him.

El Paso wasn't a big town, but it was unique in that it was the westernmost town in Texas. It was also right near the border. The law here had to coexist and work together with *el jefe* across the border in Ciudad Juarez. There were no other two towns that had the relationship these two had.

They stopped in a large cantina for a beer, admired the girls working the floor, some gringa and some Mexican.

"I think I need a woman," Charlie Utter confided to Clint. "It's been a long time."

"Don't go anywhere with one," Clint advised. "Take someone back to your room so I know where you are."

"All right," he said. "Maybe that little gal who served us our food."

"You could always ask," Clint said, although he thought Charlie would be better off with someone older, more of a pro. Also, he still didn't know what the relationship was between the girl and the bartender. It seemed personal to him, and he didn't want him or Charlie to get in the middle of that.

They left that cantina and continued to wander about El Paso until they came to the bridge to Ciudad Juarez. Clint remembered a particular gun battle that took place on that bridge.

"So we can just walk across there and be in Mexico?" Charlie asked him.

"Sure, but that's not the Mexico you want to see, Charlie," Clint said. "Stopping there would be like stopping here. You've got to ride through Juarez and just keep going."

Charlie looked at Clint.

"You decided yet if you're comin'?"

Clint didn't answer right away.

"You don't hafta, ya know," Charlie said, quickly. "I mean, I know I was in pretty sad shape when we left Socorro and you probably just rode along with me to make sure I was okay. Well, I'm okay. You don't wanna go into ol' Mexico with me, I understand."

"Well," Clint said, "I was thinking about continuing east through Texas until I come to a town called Labyrinth. It's a place I stop sometimes. You know, a place I can rest."

"A man needs his rest," Charlie said.

"You're welcome to come there with me if you want to, Charlie," Clint offered.

"Thanks, Clint," Charlie said. "But it's probably better anyway if I go off on my own. About time, I'd say. I think I got enough rest all the time I was in Socorro. I'm ready to hit the trail again on my own."

"Well, we'd better head back then, and turn in," Clint said. "I think we'll both want to get an early start tomorrow."

Steve Nash was having himself a time in bed with not one but two senoritas. One was young and slender, about eighteen with small breasts and a butt like a boy's, but the other was older—in her thirties—with big, firm breasts and a meaty ass. Nash didn't care much about the size or shape of a woman as long as she was willing. And these two were willing as long as he paid them.

For a while, he just lay on his back, looking down at the two women between his legs. Damned if the older one wasn't teaching the younger one how to suck a man's peter. It was then he realized that the young one was new at this whoring thing and the older one was breaking her in. Well, he was only too happy to help out.

"Watch me, *chiquita*," the older one said at one point. She stroked Nash's penis until it was erect, licking it occasionally just to give it an extra boost. Once he was standing tall, she took it in her mouth and sucked him wetly. Nash was not a small man, and she managed to take all of him in her mouth, which amazed not only him but the young whore as well.

"Now you try," the woman said to her.

"*Aye, dios*," the other one said, "but he is so beeg."

"*Sí*, he is a large one," the older woman said. "*Mucho* hombre. And he is prettier than most you will see here."

"Hey, ladies," Nash said, "I'm right here, and I'm blushin'."

"*Silencio*, you beautiful man," the older whore said. "We are sucking you."

Nash put his head back as the young whore took him into her mouth, and it never once occurred to the gringo that the two women were playing him to get more money out of him.

He was there for hours . . . .

When Steve Nash finally realized how long he'd been there, he bounded off the bed, paid the two woman what they asked—much more than he'd intended to spend—and then asked them where the smallest cantina in town was.

"*Calle del Sol*," the older woman said. "It is both cantina and a very fine hotel."

"Good," he said, " 'cause I'll be needin' a room, too. So long, ladies. If you ever need somebody to, ya know, use to teach any more young whores, I'd be more than willing."

"You are very kind, senor," the older woman said, tucking his money into her blouse.

As Nash left, the two women exchanged a look, rolled their eyes, then undressed again and got back into bed together.

Stupid gringo, they were both thinking.

FIFTEEN

When Clint and Charlie reentered the cantina in front of their hotel, there were only a few patrons present. The same bartender was behind the bar, scowling and cleaning the bar with a dirty rag. Clint hadn't really noticed the first time how small the place was. He supposed that the bulk of their business came from renting the rooms out—and the girls.

He didn't see the young waitress Carmen around anywhere, but there was an older woman in her thirties standing at the bar, looking bored. Her breasts, big and soft-looking, were spilling out of her low-cut top.

"Well, there's a woman for you, Charlie," he said.

"Her?" Charlie asked. "That'd be like sticking it in a cow. I wonder where that other one went to?"

"She was a little young, don't you think?"

"If they're rentin' her out, then she ain't that young," Charlie said. "Besides, what's it matter how young she is. I'm just gonna poke her, not marry 'er."

"Well then, you might as well ask for her—but ask that woman, don't ask the bartender. He looks like the kind of man who thrives on trouble."

Charlie approached the woman at the bar.

"Is Carmen around?" he asked.

She turned immediately and pulled in a deep breath so that her breasts spilled out even more.

"What's the matter, gringo?" she asked. "You no like them beeg, like me?" She put her hands beneath her breasts to illustrate her point.

"No offense, ma'am," Charlie said, "but I was askin' about the younger one."

Now the woman's face clouded. "You are saying I am too old, *cabrone*!"

Clint wasn't sure what *cabrone* meant, but he was pretty sure it wasn't anything good.

Charlie looked over at Clint, as if for help. Clint sighed and stepped forward.

"Senorita," he said, "my friend meant no disrespect to you."

She tossed her hair and gave both men a hurt look.

"Are you insultin' my wife?" the bartender demanded.

His wife? Clint wondered what a man who apparently hated everything Mexican was doing with a Mexican wife.

"Nobody was insulting anybody," Clint said, hastily. He noticed the bartender's hand was beneath the bar. He either had a club there or, worse, a gun—maybe even a shotgun.

"You sayin' my wife ain't a good enough whore for you?" the man asked Charlie.

"He was just—" Clint started, but the bartender would not let him get the words out.

"I ain't askin' you," the man said, "I'm askin' him."

"I'm sure she's great—" Charlie said.

"You bet she is," the bartender said. "She's the best whore in town. Look at them tits." The man reached out with his left hand—the right still suspiciously beneath the bar—and pulled down his wife's blouse so that both huge breasts bobbed free. He then grabbed one and squeezed it, allowing the nipple to pop out between two fingers.

There were only a couple of other men still in the cantina, and both of their eyes bugged out at the sight of the woman's naked breasts.

"Look, mister," Charlie said, "all I was askin' is where that other gal was. Uh, Carmen, I think her name was."

"Carmen?" the bartender asked. He released his hold on his wife's breast, and she didn't bother to cover them. "That skinny little bitch?"

"Now, there ain't no cause to talk that way," Charlie said. "What's the difference to you, anyhow? If I go with your wife, or Carmen, don't you still get the money?"

"Sure I do," the man said. He narrowed his eyes, then seemed to come up with a thought. "Well, Carmen's extra, ya know, because she's so young."

"Sure, that's fine," Charlie said, "whatever."

"You'll have ta wait until she's finished in the back," the bartender said. "She's got another customer, right now. When she's done I'll send her to your room."

"That's fine."

"What about you?" the bartender asked Clint. "You interested in this one?" He reached out and pinched one of her nipples. She laughed, even though it looked to Clint like it hurt.

"No, thanks," Clint said, wondering how he could put this so they wouldn't get insulted. "I'm a little too tired, and I think this gal here would probably just kill me."

The bartender found that funny. He laughed loudly, and too long, but at least he brought his other hand into sight, empty.

"That's a good one," he said. "You're probably right. Theresa would probably kill you."

"Okay, then," Clint said. "We got that settled." He clapped Charlie on the shoulder. "He'll send the other gal to your room when she's done."

Charlie nodded, apparently satisfied.

"Well, whataya think, woman?" the bartender asked Theresa as Clint and Charlie headed for their rooms. "The gringos are starting to prefer our daughter to you."

"Maybe the little *puta* will make us enough money so that I can retire," Theresa said, "and be only with you, *mi amor*."

"Retire?" the bartender said. "What are you, crazy? You got ten or fifteen more good years in you . . ."

Clint didn't hear the rest. His head was still spinning now that he realized the couple was pimping their own daughter. He wondered if Charlie had heard the remark.

Steve Nash was still looking at the whore's tits when she tucked them back into her blouse. Once they were out of sight, he looked over at Clint Adams and Charlie Utter, catching them just before she stepped out of sight into the hallway of the hotel.

Jesus, he thought, if Del and the others had walked in during the past ten minutes, there woulda been a helluva shoot-out in that place. What a coincidence that the smallest cantina in the town also had a hotel behind it where Clint Adams was staying!

For a minute there, while the bartender had his hand out of sight beneath the bar, Nash thought he was going to get to see the Gunsmith in action, but the man had joked his way out of it. The Gunsmith. Huh. Didn't seem like much to him. Climbs out a window to avoid one fight, and makes jokes to avoid another one. What kind of legend was that?

Nash decided to go outside and wait for Virtue and the others out there, just in case Adams decided to come back out. He wanted to be able to warn the others before anything happened. He knew that Del Virtue was not a man who liked surprises.

SIXTEEN

As Clint and Charlie walked back to their rooms, they could hear a man grunting and a bed creaking. They could not hear a woman. That led Clint to believe that the woman they'd heard screaming earlier was probably the mother, not the daughter.

They came to Clint's room first and he stopped.

"Enjoy yourself," he told Charlie.

Charlie didn't say anything. He kept walking down to his room and entered. Maybe he was just too excited about being with the young girl to have heard him. Or maybe he was having second thoughts. Whatever it was, it was his business, not Clint's.

He opened the door to his own room and went inside.

Out front Steve Nash was smoking a cigar and waiting for the rest of his gang to arrive. As he pulled over a flimsy wooden chair to sit on, two men approached the cantina and he realized he knew them.

"Harry?" he said. "Harry Thorpe?"

Thorpe, a man in his thirties, just a couple of years older than Nash, stopped, stared, then smiled.

"Steve Nash, you son of a bitch," he said. "What the hell are you doing in El Paso?"

"I'm ridin' with Del Virtue," Nash said. "We got somethin' goin' here in town."

Thorpe looked at his companion, a man roughly the same age.

"This is Ernie Pitt," he said. "He's a good man. You think Del needs a couple more men?"

"I don't know," Nash said. "What're you two doin' in El Paso?"

"We're just passin' through," Pitt said. "Not sure if we should take a look at Mexico or keep headin' east."

"Well, look," Nash said, "Del's due here any minute with the rest of the men."

"How many?" Thorpe asked.

"There's five of us all together. I don't know if Del's gonna want to use any more, though. Why don't you tell me where you're stayin', and I'll let you know."

"Well," Thorpe said, "we were about to go in here."

"I wouldn't recommend it," Nash said. "I just came out of there."

"Good enough for you, but not us?" Pitt asked.

"That's not it," Nash said. "I ain't stayin' here. Del and me just agreed we'd meet at the smallest cantina in town, and this is it. There's another one just down the street. Why don't you go down there and wait. Shouldn't be much longer."

"It better be tonight," Thorpe said.

"It's gonna be in the next hour," Nash said. "Then when I tell him what I know, he'll decide."

"Is there a lot of money at stake here?" Pitt asked.

Nash hesitated. If he told them that all Virtue really wanted to do was kill the Gunsmith, it might have scared them off. And to tell the truth, he didn't know if killing the Gunsmith would translate into a lot of money in the future.

"I think only Del knows what he's plannin' and how

good it is," Nash said. "Me, I just do what I'm told and count my share."

Thorpe and Pitt exchanged a glance, then shrugged. Thorpe said, "Okay, we'll go over to that other cantina and wait a couple of hours."

"If you don't hear from me by then," Nash said, "it was nice seein' you again."

As the two men turned and went off up the street, Nash thought that if it was up to him he wouldn't mind having two more guns on their side when they faced the Gunsmith, but it was not up to him, it was up to Del Virtue.

He noticed that his cigar had gone out. Sitting back down, he lit it again, got the tip glowing and sat back to wait. He was glad that he didn't have to make any decisions. He was happy to leave that to others. He'd taken orders from men before Del Virtue, and he'd take orders after Del Virtue was gone, all the while doing whatever was right for Steve Nash.

SEVENTEEN

By the time Del Virtue and the others rode up in front of the cantina, Nash was finished with his cigar. He got out of his chair and walked to the edge of the boardwalk to greet them.

"Can't we go in and get a drink?" Horrigan asked Nash. "You gotta meet us outside."

"You're not gonna believe this, Del," Nash said. "This place is also a hotel, and guess who has rooms here?"

"I don't think I have to guess," Virtue said. "Adams and that friend of Hickok's?"

"That's right."

"One room or two?"

"Two."

"Anybody with them?"

"Hickok's friend is supposed to have a whore with him."

"Which rooms are they in?"

"That I don't know."

"How many rooms in the hotel?"

"Don't know," Nash said, "but it ain't a big place."

Virtue leaned forward in his saddle. "You were sup-

69

posed to have all the information we needed, Steve," he said.

"I do, Del," Nash said. "They're inside."

Virtue leaned back. It wasn't late and the cantina was still open for business. "What kind of business they do in there?" he asked.

"Not much," Nash said. "The bartender's got hisself two whores—get this, his wife and his daughter."

"There's an enterprising fella," Virtue said. "All right, let's get these horses away from here. We'll come back on foot, catch them in their rooms."

"You don't wanna wait for them to come out?" Horrigan asked.

"No, not this time," Virtue said. "This time we're just gonna go in after Adams."

"And what about the other fella?" Neal Jones asked.

"If he gets in the way, he gets killed, too," Virtue said, "but we go for Adams, first."

"Should we take the horses to a stable?" Horrigan asked.

"No," Virtue said, "I just don't want them in front of here. We'll leave them down the street."

"I'll walk along with you, Del," Nash said. "I got somethin' to ask you about these two fellas I know . . ."

The bartender and owner of the cantina and hotel was named Jerry Dunworthy.

"Are they gone?" he asked his wife, Theresa.

She was looking out the front window and turned away from it to answer him.

"*Sí*, they are gone."

"Who were they?"

"I do not know," she said, "just a bunch of gringos."

"Is Carmen with the blond man?"

"Yes."

"And the other?"

"In his room."

There was only one other man in the place as they spoke. At this time of night the other, bigger cantinas had more to offer people in the way of entertainment. That suited Dunworthy just fine. He didn't need people around when he was conducting his real business.

"Wake Chulo," he told her, indicating the sleeping man. "Send him for the others."

"And tell them what?"

"What else?" he said. "Tell them that we have two more rich gringos in our hotel."

EIGHTEEN

"I don't think we'll need two more men," Del Virtue told Steve Nash as they all walked back toward the cantina. "I think we got enough men to get the job done."

"What about after this job is done?" Nash asked. "They're two pretty good boys."

"After we get this done, there's gonna be lots of pretty good boys who are gonna want to ride with us," Virtue said. "Let's just concentrate on the job at hand, Steve."

"Hold it!" Neal Jones said, stopping their progress.

"What?" Virtue asked.

"What is goin' on there?" Jones asked, pointing.

They all looked ahead at the cantina and saw a group of men going inside with their guns drawn.

"They're gonna beat us to it," Horrigan said. "Somebody must've told them—"

"Nobody told 'em nothin'," Virtue said. "They're a bunch of bandidos, looking for easy pickin's."

"They ain't gonna find that with Clint Adams," Nash pointed out.

"This oughtta be good," Virtue said. "Let's watch."

"And then what?" Horrigan asked.

"We'll go in and pick up the pieces."

• • •

When the soft knock came at Charlie Utter's door, his stomach jumped. He opened the door, feeling like a fool boy going to his first dance with a girl.

"Senor," the young Mexican girl said, "you want me?"

"Hell, yes," Charlie said, thickly.

"You must pay," she said, "or my *papi*, he will beat me."

"I'll pay," Charlie promised her. "Don't worry, I've got plenty of money. Ain't nobody gonna beat ya."

She smiled and said, "Then I will come in."

He stepped out of the way to let her in, and as she slipped past him he closed the door, then turned. What he saw froze him in his tracks. Somehow she had already shucked her clothes and was standing there naked. She sure didn't have the same body as her *mami*. She was slender, small-breasted, but those big brown nipples were pointing right at him.

She stepped close to him and he could smell her. She had not come to him straight from another man's bed. She had washed herself. Even her hair smelled fragrant.

She reached between his legs and felt him through his trousers.

"*Aye*," she said softly, squeezing, "we must let the monster be free."

Clint was in his room lying on the thin mattress of his bed, thinking it was hardly better than the ground. The more he looked around the room, the more he knew they'd made a mistake. This was not a hotel to stay in, it was just a place to come and have a girl. But it was too late to do anything about that now. They'd paid, and Charlie *was* getting a girl. So he might as well just try and get to sleep—except it was quiet.

Too quiet.

He should have heard some commotion from the cantina, or at least the older whore—the mother with the huge breasts—screaming from one of the other rooms.

But he wasn't hearing anything.

He got off the bed and crept toward the door.

Jerry Dunworthy pointed down the hall and said to the five bandidos, one of whom was Theresa's brother, "Rooms seven and nine."

"Which one first?" Jerry's brother-in-law Ricardo asked.

"Nine," Jerry said. "That is the gringo who is with Carmen."

It was Theresa who grabbed Ricardo's arm tightly. "And don't shoot my daughter."

"Do not worry," Ricardo said. "I would not shoot my own niece." Then he grinned. "I might have some use for her myself after this is over."

"You'll have to pay," Jerry said, "just like anybody else. We don't have no special prices for family."

"I will pay," Ricardo said, "from my share."

"I saw the smaller gringo with an envelope full of money," Theresa told her brother. "But the other one must have some money, too."

"If they have money," Ricardo wondered aloud, "why are they staying here?"

"The smaller gringo took one look at our Carmen," Theresa said, "and he was lost."

"And I know why," Ricardo said, once again revealing several gold teeth in a grin that crossed over into a leer.

A couple of the other bandidos were waiting for the conversation to end, and while they waited they ogled Theresa's breasts.

"Tell your men to stop lookin' at my wife like that," Jerry said, "unless they're willin' to pay."

"They will pay," Ricardo said. "We will all pay."

"Yeah, well," Jerry said, "not until you get this job done, ya know?"

"Be calm, my friend," Ricardo said. "The job will get done.

"*Muchachos*," he snapped at his men. "*Andale!*"

NINETEEN

Clint pressed his ear to the door, listening for sounds in the hallway outside. First there was nothing, then a rustling, some whispers, and finally a muttered curse. It was enough to tell him that something was going on.

He opened the door quietly, just a crack, just as the last of the bandidos was going by. If they had chosen to hit his room before Charlie's, there might have been a different outcome. He waited for the last man to go by, then swung the door open and stepped out into the hall, drawing his gun.

"Charlieeeeee!" he shouted just as the first bandido hit Charlie's door with a well-placed kick. There was an immediate shot, and the man went flying across the hall.

The remaining four men were unsure of which way to turn as Charlie came out into the hall, gun in hand. Clint immediately moved to his left, flattening himself against the wall as he fired. He did not want to chance shooting Charlie. The bandidos tried to bring their weapons to bear, but they were caught in a deadly cross fire that cut them down in moments. When the hall fell quiet, Clint could see that Charlie, too, had taken a precaution against accidentally shooting Clint—he had gone down to one knee. Gun smoke filled the air in the hall, rising and dissipating. Clint quickly reloaded, aware of Charlie's empty shells hitting the floor as he did the same.

"You were ready," Clint said, as they converged over the fallen bodies.

"That little gal was just a tad too eager and attentive," Charlie said. "I figured somethin' was up."

"I figure her daddy was behind this, but we'll have a hell of a time proving it."

At that moment Carmen stuck her head out the door, took one look at the carnage, then centered her attention on the first man Charlie had shot and shouted, "*Tio* Ricardo!"

"*Tio*?" Charlie asked Clint.

"Uncle, I think," Clint translated.

"Uncle? What the hell kinda family is this?"

"Speaking of family," Clint said, "I wonder where Mom and Dad are."

"You killed him," Carmen said, her hand red with the blood of her uncle.

They ignored her.

"You'd think if they were so innocent in all this they'd come running to see what the commotion was," Clint commented.

"You killed them all!" Carmen shouted.

"Yeah, well, they were all tryin' to kill us, sweetheart," Charlie said. "While you were tryin' ta keep me busy in bed."

"You were paying for it," Carmen said, sticking out her bottom lip.

"Well, I won't make that mistake again."

"I guess we'd better get ready to receive the sheriff," Clint said.

"This looks easy enough to explain," Charlie said, indicating the carnage in the hall.

"Let's hope so."

Both men had turned their attention away from Carmen,

who took the opportunity to pick up her uncle's gun, cock the hammer and turn the weapon their way.

Both Charlie and Clint heard the weapon cock, and then Charlie shouted, "Clint, watch out!"

There was a shot, and a burning pain in Clint's side, and then Charlie drew his gun and fired . . .

Outside, Del Virtue and his men heard all the shooting from inside the hotel.

"Looks like somebody did our work for us, Del," Horrigan said. "We're shit out of luck."

"Not so fast, Ben," Virtue said. "We're gonna stick around and find out what happened."

"Whataya think happened?" Horrigan asked. "They caught the Gunsmith sleepin' and blasted him."

"Sounds to me like gunfire and return gunfire," Steve Nash said.

"Yeah," Virtue said, "me, too."

"How can you tell—" Horrigan started, but there was another lone gunshot that silenced him.

"I wonder what that was?" Neal Jones said.

"We're gonna stay right here until we find out," Del Virtue said.

TWENTY

"Okay," Sheriff Tom Paxton said, "I can see where you had to kill the men. It's pretty obvious what they had in mind when they were sneaking down the hall with their guns out. But . . . tell me again why you had to kill the young girl, Carmen?"

Paxton was in his mid-thirties and had been wearing a badge in El Paso for less than six months. He had finally responded to the shooting with two deputies, then sent one of them for a doctor when he saw that Clint had been shot.

Now they were in Clint's room. His trousers were down around his ankles while the doctor dug a bullet out of his hip.

"I tol' you, Sheriff," Charlie Utter said. "She picked up one of the guns and shot Clint. She woulda shot him again—or me—if I hadn't stopped her."

"But . . . you had to shoot her?"

"She was shootin' Clint in the back!" Charlie said. His eyes were kind of wild. "I couldn't let that happen—again!"

"Again?"

The sheriff looked at Clint.

"Charlie and Bill Hickock were friends."

"Oh."

"Come on, Doc," Clint said. "I could have gotten that bullet out faster myself."

"I should go ahead and let you try, young man," the doctor said. He was white-haired, in his sixties, and he shook. One of two doctors in town, he was the one the sheriff's office called when they needed a sawbones.

"Mr. Adams, ya gotta excuse me," the sheriff said, "but you're the Gunsmith. You couldn't figure out another way to stop the girl than shootin' her between the eyes?"

"First of all," Clint said, grimacing as the doctor probed, "why do I have to excuse you?"

"Uh, well—"

"Second of all, I had my back to the girl. Charlie was the only one with a chance to stop her before she shot me again."

"Her parents are gonna be real upset."

"Her parents have probably left town!" Clint said. "They've been running a whorehouse back here and have probably robbed and killed more men than you can count. Once they realized we had killed their men, they probably lit out."

"I know Jerry and Theresa," the sheriff said. "They wouldn't just leave their business."

"Then where are they?" Clint asked Paxton. "Wouldn't you think they'd be curious about shots being fired in their place? Unless, of course, they expected it."

"So you're sayin' that Jerry sent these men back here to rob and kill you?" the lawman asked.

"That's my best guess, Sheriff," Clint said. "What's yours?"

"Got it!" the doctor said. The chunk of lead dropped into the basin of water he had near the bed. "The wound actually isn't too bad. I'll clean it and bandage it."

"So I'll live?" Clint asked.

"Providing you don't get on a horse anytime soon and bleed to death," the doctor said, "yes."

"How long before I can ride?"

"Depends on what a good healer you are," the doctor said. "I'd say weeks."

"Damn it!"

Clint was angry at himself for getting caught this way. It was not only foolish, but stupid to have ignored the distraught girl.

"Doc, is Clint gonna need rest?" Charlie asked.

"Lots of it," the doctor said, cleaning the wound.

Charlie turned on the sheriff. "That's all, Sheriff," he said. "If you wanna talk to Clint any more it'll have to be in the mornin'."

"Are you two . . . stayin' here?" the lawman asked.

"Why not? We paid for the rooms."

"But . . . if Jerry and Theresa ain't around—"

"Then they took off with our money," Clint said. "You should be looking for them."

"And gettin' that girl's body out of the hallway," the doc added.

"My men have taken the dead men over to the undertaker's, Doc," Paxton said, "but where do I take the girl?"

"Take her to the undertaker, as well," the doc said, applying a bandage to Clint's wound. "If her parents show up, tell them where she is."

Paxton took off his hat, scratched his head, then put it back on.

"If you're worried about this man taking off on you, forget it," the doctor said. "He'll be in bed for days."

Paxton looked at Charlie.

"I ain't goin' nowhere until Clint can ride."

"You'd better not," Paxton said. "I got more questions—"

"They'll have to wait until mornin', Sheriff," Charlie said. "Time for you to go and clean up the rest of the mess in the hall."

"All right," Paxton said, "but I'll be back in the mornin'."

"We'll be here," Clint said, wincing as the doctor finished his ministrations.

"I'm done here, Tom," the doctor said, standing up.

"You'll come back and check on him, won't ya, Doc?" Charlie asked.

"In a couple of days," the old doctor said. "Meanwhile, he'll need somebody to change that bandage and keep the wound clean so it doesn't get infected."

"I've taken care of bullet wounds before," Charlie said.

"Okay, then." The doctor looked at the sheriff.

"Just remember," the lawman said before leaving, "I'll be back in the morning."

"So you said," Charlie replied, and closed the door behind them.

"You saved my life, Charlie," Clint said. "Don't be too upset about shooting that gal."

"I know," Charlie said. "There wasn't much else I coulda done, but it still don't sit right with me."

"You can do me a favor—actually, you can do both of us a favor."

"What's that?"

"Get a bottle of whiskey from the bar," Clint said, "and on the way back check and see if any of the other rooms are occupied. You should know if we got company for the night."

"Both of those sound like good ideas," Charlie said. "I'll be right back."

Virtue and his men watched the sheriff and his deputies run into the building, then saw them carry bodies out one by one—none of them the body of the Gunsmith.

"They all look like bandidos to me," Nash said. "What do you think Del?"

"Looks like it."

Finally, they carried out the body of a girl.

"Looks like a whore caught a bullet also," Jones said.

"Steve," Virtue said, "see that sawbones comin' out with the sheriff?"

"I see 'em."

"Find out what he knows, who he treated."

"Okay. Where will you be?"

"Down the street. You said there was another cantina?"

"Yep."

"And your two friends are in there?"

"Should be."

"Tell me their names again," Virtue said. "I'm thinking we might need a little more help."

"Why are we gonna need more help?" Horrigan asked.

"Because we just watched the local law carry five bandidos out of that hotel," Virtue said.

"We don't know that Adams killed them."

"Steve's gonna find out what happened from the doctor," Virtue said. "Go ahead, Steve."

"Right."

As Nash left, Virtue said, "Meanwhile, we're gonna have some drinks, and find us some rooms."

"Rooms?" Horrigan asked.

"Yep, looks to me like we'll be here a mite longer than we thought."

TWENTY-ONE

"Hotel's empty," Charlie said, when he reentered Clint's room. "So's the cantina. I locked the doors."

"So we've got the whole place to ourselves?"

"Looks like." Charlie held up the bottle of whiskey.

"Hand it over."

Charlie took off the top and passed the bottle to Clint, who took a couple of good swallows and handed it back.

"I don't usually drink whiskey, but I think I'm going to need it to sleep," he explained.

"You go ahead," Charlie said, taking a small swallow of his own. "I'll stand watch."

"I was hoping you'd say that."

"You don't have to worry about a thing, Clint," Charlie promised. "I'll watch your back."

"You already did," Clint said. "It's the only reason I'm still alive to even drink. I owe you big, Charlie."

Charlie handed him the bottle again.

"I'll set up out in the hall," he said. "There's a back door, but I locked it. Might look into barricading it, too."

Clint took three long, deep swallows of whiskey that

87

made his eyes start to water. He passed the bottle back to Charlie, then let himself flop down on his back.

Charlie took the bottle out into the hall with him.

When Steve Nash entered the cantina, he saw Neal Jones, Ben Horrigan and Mark Connors standing at the bar. When he looked around the room, he saw Del Virtue sitting at a table with Harry Thorpe and Ernie Pitt. He walked over and joined them.

"Hey, Steve," Thorpe said. "You didn't tell us the Gun-smith was involved in your play."

"Not my place to tell, Harry."

"Thorpe and Pitt are gonna join us, Steve."

"Fine."

"That was a good call on your part."

"Thanks."

"Why don't you boys go to the bar and get acquainted with the others?" Virtue suggested.

"Sure thing, Del," Thorpe said. He and Pitt got up and left the table.

"What'd you find out from the doc?"

"They gunned five men in the hallway," Nash said. "Doc said it didn't look like any of the bandidos even got off a shot."

"Looks like the Gunsmith just might be livin' up to his reputation," Virtue said. "What else?"

"Adams took a bullet in the hip."

"That's interesting," Virtue said. "If the bandits didn't get off a shot, who got him?"

"Get this," Nash said. "An eighteen-year-old whore grabbed a gun and plugged him from behind."

Virtue whistled soundlessly.

"What happened to the whore?"

"Charlie Utter shot her," Nash said. "Right between the eyes."

"Who owns that place?"

"Fella named Jerry Dunworthy. Him and his whore wife, Theresa, are the dead girl's parents."

"And where are they?"

"The law's wonderin' the same thing," Nash said. "Adams figures this Jerry and his wife fingered him for the bandidos. Figures that's what their business really was."

"And they're gone?"

"In the wind, looks like."

"Real concerned parents, them two."

Nash didn't think that called for an answer from him.

"Okay," Virtue said, "does the doc know how many other people are in that hotel?"

"He says none," Nash replied. "The place is empty except for Adams and Utter."

Virtue digested that information and Nash waited. He never even wondered what Virtue was going to decide to do. Decisions just weren't his job. Whatever Del said to do, he'd do.

"Okay," Virtue said, "take one of the others and go have a look at the place. Front door, back door, windows. The roof. The works."

"Okay. Who should I take?"

Virtue thought a moment, then said, "Take one of your friends."

"They're not friends," Nash said. "I know Harry Thorpe, only met Ernie Pitt today. I know Thorpe, but I never said we was friends. I only said he was a good hand."

"Okay, then," Virtue said, "take the good hand with you and check the place out."

"Where will you and the boys be?"

"You got a hotel room yet?" Virtue asked.

"No," Nash said, "I was waitin' to see what you wanted to do."

"We're gonna get rooms," Virtue said. "I saw a place down the block, real hotel with two floors. We'll get you one, too. After that, I'll be right here, waitin' on you."

"Okay, boss," Nash said. "I'll see you later."

Virtue watched Nash collect Thorpe from the bar and the two men left. He liked Nash best of all the man he worked with. The man never questioned him, just did as he was told. Ben Horrigan could take a lesson from Nash. In fact, he should take a lesson, because if he didn't change his behavior pretty quick, he wasn't going to last much longer.

TWENTY-TWO

"Why don't we just go in and get them?" Thorpe asked, on the way to the cantina and hotel. "There's seven of us and only two of them, right?"

"I don't know," Nash said. "That's up to Del."

"Don't you ever ask him any questions?" Thorpe asked. "Make any suggestions?"

"Nope."

"Why not?"

"He's the boss," Nash said. "He makes all the decisions."

"Don't you ever think you got a better idea than he does?"

"No."

"Whatsamatter, Steve?" Thorpe asked. "Don't you ever wanna be your own boss?"

"No, and if you do," Nash replied, "then maybe you shouldn't be throwin' in with us."

"Oh, I don't mean now," Thorpe said. "I'm happy to let Virtue make all the decisions now. I mean somewhere down the road. You don't ever wanna be your own boss?"

"No."

"Why not?"

"It's too much trouble bein' the boss," Nash said.

"Everybody looks at you for everything, every decision. I don't want that. I'm happy just doin' what I'm told. I'm good at it."

Thorpe hesitated a moment, then said, "Well, if you've found somethin' you're good at . . ."

They reached the cantina and stopped just across the street.

"You want the front or the back?" Nash asked.

"I'll take the back," Thorpe said. "We just checking for ways in, if they're locked or not."

"That's right."

"And then we'll meet up later in front?"

"Right."

Thorpe chuckled.

"What?"

"You really stay away from makin' any decisions, don't ya?"

"Yeah, I do. My life is a lot simpler that way."

"Well," Thorpe said, slapping Nash on the back, "who am I to argue with that?"

The two men separated, fading off into the dark shadows around the building.

Charlie thought he heard something, drew his gun and stood very still, listening. Yup, it sounded like somebody was moving around outside the building. He crept down the hallway to the back door, which he had barricaded using some furniture from the empty rooms. He stopped again to listen. It sounded like somebody was moving around out there, and then someone tried the doorknob. Charlie moved to a window in one of the darkened rooms off the hall. There was enough moonlight outside for him to see the silhouette of someone moving. Somebody had sent this man to check out the building. Maybe he even had some help, somebody checking the front, as well. Charlie felt sure they were just on a reconnaissance mission, but he left the dark room and ran down the hall to the front of the cantina. The place was dark and he moved to a window. Sure enough he saw a man outside, checking the front of the building. They'd be checking the sides next, but Charlie had already made sure that all the windows were locked. And just in case they managed to get in through a window anyway, he'd taken the room keys and locked all the doors from the outside.

He went back up the hall to Clint's room, where'd he'd set a chair for himself right outside the door. Even if anybody got in, they were going to have to go through him to get to Clint Adams.

He wasn't about to lose another friend.

Not that way.

Nash and Thorpe regrouped at the front.

"Anything?" Nash asked.

"Everything's locked up tight," Harry Thorpe told him. "Doors and windows."

"Yeah, that's what I found. No side doors."

"Just front and back."

"Could you get to the roof?"

"If I had to," Thorpe said. "The building's only one story. But they'd hear us walking up there."

"That's what I figured."

"So I guess we'd better go back and tell Virtue what we found, huh?" Thorpe asked.

"I guess so."

Charlie watched from the front window as the two men converged, then turned and walked away. They had checked everything but the roof. He'd left his chair as an afterthought to check the front again, which is the only reason he was able to see both men. But he hadn't seen either of them well enough to be able to tell if he knew them, from Socorro or anywhere else. He turned and went back to his chair. He didn't think anyone else would be bothering them that night.

TWENTY-THREE

Charlie woke with a start the next morning and almost fell off his chair. He'd had it leaning back against Clint's door so nobody could get past him. It never occurred to him what might happen if Clint had tried to get out.

He stood up, stretched to get the kinks out from sleeping in a chair all night. He moved the chair then and opened Clint's door as quietly as he could. The deep, easy breathing told him that his friend was still asleep—and, more importantly, still alive.

He closed the door, leaving himself out in the hall again. He was suddenly hungry, but knew he couldn't leave the building to get something to eat. He decided to go and find the kitchen and see what he could do himself.

When Clint woke, he felt feverish. He knew, however, that his wound had not become infected, because he'd had that experience before and it was usually accompanied by a distinctly putrid odor. The fever was just a by-product of being shot.

He shifted in bed, waiting for the pain, but when it came it was bearable. Apparently the doctor had been correct, the wound was not serious. Still, Clint knew that mounting

95

a horse too soon could turn it serious. He'd take the doctor's advice and not try to ride, but rather than waiting weeks, he'd wait a few days. He was a good judge of what his body could do after all these years. After all, this was not the first time he'd been shot.

He came awake in stages. That was because of the whiskey he drank the night before. As his senses came alive, he thought he could smell food. Suddenly, he was ravenous, almost to the point of pain. He decided to risk getting to his feet so he could follow his nose.

Del Virtue woke alone in his own room. The rest of his men had to share rooms, but he always made sure he had his own.

He'd waited in the cantina last night until Nash returned with his friend Thorpe. They told him that the building that housed the cantina and hotel where Clint Adams was staying was like a small fortress. Front door, back door, both locked tightly. Of course, windows would be easy to break, but the breaking glass would alert Adams and his friend.

Virtue had two choices. He could wait for Adams to come out on his own, or go in after him. He'd made the mistake of waiting in Magdalena—although the big mistake there was in not covering the back. Who imagined that Clint Adams, the Gunsmith, would sneak out the back?

He got out of bed and walked to the window to look down at El Paso. Adams's gunshot wound would keep him in town for a while. Before he decided what to do, he was going to have to check out the local law and see if they were going to be a problem.

The other problem was that Adams and his friend, Utter, had gunned down five bandidos. Virtue now had—counting himself and the two new men—a force of seven. He had to decide if that was enough and, if not, was El Paso a place where he could recruit capable men?

Steve Nash was the man who usually did all his reconnaissance, but he decided to check out the local law himself, right after breakfast.

The main problem that came out of being shot was that Clint could not strap on his holster. He worried that the belt could irritate the wound, so he slung the holster over his shoulder and left his room. The pants he was wearing had a hole and dried blood on them, but they were all he had. He'd see about buying a new pair later.

He left his room, stepped into the hall and encountered the definite smell of something cooking. Following his nose down the hall and through the cantina, he found his way to the kitchen where he was surprised to find Charlie Utter standing at the steaming stove.

"Charlie?"

Utter turned his head at the sound of Clint's voice, looking surprised. "Clint? What are you doin' up?"

"The doctor was right. The wound isn't that bad," Clint explained. "What are you doing?"

"I was hungry, figured I couldn't go out for breakfast, and thought that since we had the whole place to ourselves I might as well use the kitchen. I found the makings for Mexican food, probably tacos and enchiladas, but since I can't make them I'm doin' the best I can." He pointed to the skillet on the stove. "Meat and beans."

"We roll that up into tortillas and we'll have tacos," Clint said.

"And in this pan"—he pointed to another one—"eggs."

"Sounds good to me. I'm starving."

There was a wooden table and two chairs off to one side, so Charlie said, "Have a seat there. I made coffee. It won't be as good as yours, but it's hot and black."

"Good enough."

Clint limped over to the table and settled himself gently into one of the chairs. He had to lean to one side to keep the pressure off his wounded hip, but it was comfortable enough.

Charlie brought him a cup and the pot.

"I saw a couple of shadows creepin' around the buildin' last night," he said, returning to the stove.

"Any faces?"

"Naw," Charlie said, "but they was checkin' the buildin' to see how hard it would be to get in."

"And how hard would it be?"

"Well, we can put up barricades and lock the doors to all the rooms so it don't matter if they get in a window," Charlie explained. "I think we can hold out here for a while."

"And then what?" Clint asked. "I think we know the law's not going to be helpful to us."

Charlie scraped the contents of both pans into two plates and carried them both to the table. Then he got himself a cup and a fork for each of them and sat down. Clint poured him a cup of coffee.

"I'm back where I was in Magdalena," he said, "only I'm stuck with you instead of a naked saloon girl."

"That don't sound so good."

"And I was on the second floor there, which was harder to get to," Clint added.

"You think it's the same fellas as back there?"

"I don't know," Clint said. "I guess we could try to figure it out. Maybe that fella who owns this place—Jerry— has still got some bandido friends."

"Or family," Charlie added.

"Right. And he's going to try to use them to get his place back."

"This is his place," Charlie said. "It belongs to him. Why does he have to try to get it back?"

"I'm not talking legally, I'm just saying he may want to reclaim it without having to face us."

"I getcha. We know he sent those bandidos after us, we just can't prove it. The law will be on his side."

"Right, but we're on the other side, and he won't face us."

"Or," Charlie said, "him and his whore wife have left

town, and we got some other fellas lookin' to try their luck."

"Word gets around what happened—especially the fact that I got shot by a girl—and all of a sudden we're fair game."

"Right."

"Wrong," Clint said. "I'm fair game. You could probably walk out of here, Charlie."

"And why would I do that?"

"I don't think anybody would stop you."

"That would leave you here alone."

"I know that."

"Well, I know it, too, Clint, and I ain't gonna do it, so get that thought outta your head right now, pard."

"Okay," Clint said, "what if you just walk out to find out what's going on? Find out who was checking this place out?"

"That still leaves you here alone."

"If they were just going to come busting in, they would have done that by now," Clint pointed out. "I think we got time for you to get the lay of the land."

Charlie scratched his head.

"Lemme think it over for a while. Why don't you just quiet down and eat your breakfast?"

Clint decided to take the advice and tucked into his meat and beans and eggs. Whatever it was called, it was delicious.

TWENTY-FOUR

Over breakfast they tried to work out a plan. Actually, there was no "they" involved, since Del Virtue would be making all the decisions.

Virtue had gone down to find a place for breakfast and had run into Steve Nash and Neal Jones in front of the hotel. They decided to eat together and found a small café a few blocks away. They all ordered steak and eggs and sat at a back table.

"You decide what we're gonna do today, Del?" Jones asked.

"I'm gonna go see the sheriff," he said. "I wanna find out if he's gonna be a problem for us."

"What about Adams?"

"We're gonna have our new friends, Thorpe and Pitt, watch the building to see if he tries to leave," Virtue said. "But according to Steve, here, the doctor told Adams he'd bleed to death if he tried to ride."

"That's right," Nash said.

"So we're gonna assume that Adams is gonna be laid up for a while," Virtue said.

"In other words," Jones said, "A sittin' duck."

Virtue smiled. "Exactly."

•   •   •

After breakfast Clint and Charlie walked around the building, checking the windows in each individual room. The rooms were dirty, for the most part, obviously not to be used for a long-term stay.

"We bought in for trouble when we decided to stay here," Clint said. "We should have looked at some other hotels, but it's too late now. We're here, and we're stuck."

"At least until you heal."

"Or until they—whoever they are—come in for us."

"What about the sheriff?"

"You saw the same man I did," Clint said. "What do you think?"

"He won't be much help."

"We're on our own," Clint said. "It would help if we knew who we were dealing with, and how many."

"So I have to find out."

"I can't," Clint said. "My hip keeps me from being on my feet for a long period of time and besides, I think they'd probably shoot me on sight if I walked out."

"But not me?"

"Let's go back to my room and talk about that," Clint said. "My leg is starting to give out."

By the time they reached his room, Clint was leaning on Charlie for support. Once he was on the bed, Charlie looked at the window in the room.

"I think the first thing we need to do is board up that window."

"Might be some nails and a hammer in a storeroom."

"I'll check," Charlie said. "We can talk while I'm nailing it shut."

He was gone for about fifteen minutes, then returned with some boards, a hammer and some nails.

"Sure enough, this stuff was in the storeroom."

It took a matter of minutes for him to nail some boards

over the window so that no one could see in or, more importantly, shoot in.

"Okay," Clint said, "let's talk about you going outside."

"What do they have ta gain by shootin' me?" Charlie asked. "It ain't gonna help anybody's reputation."

"It'll leave me alone to face them, though," Clint pointed out.

Charlie rubbed his jaw.

"I wish we knew who they were," he said, "and if they been watchin' us long enough to recognize me."

"I'm worried about the horses," Clint said. "It would be smart of them to grab our mounts."

"You know," Charlie said, "the best thing might be to go out and face them and get it over with."

"Not without knowing how many," Clint said, "and not for a few days, at least, until I can stand better and longer."

"So we're back to findin' out who they are, and how many," Charlie observed, "and that falls to me."

"You know," Clint said, "the sheriff won't back any play we make, but he might be helpful in answering those questions."

"I guess I could start there."

"Now all you have to do is get out of the building."

"Back way seems the best bet," Charlie said, "but first I'll have a look in the back and front to see if we're bein' watched."

"We might be blowing this way out of proportion, too," Clint said. "Once word gets around that we handled those five bandidos, it might actually be that nobody wants to have anything to do with us."

"One way or the other," Charlie said, "I got to go outside and find out some things."

"I'm sorry this falls on you, Charlie."

"It don't matter," Charlie said. "I'm still the one least likely to be shot on sight. Somebody might try to pick a fight with me, but I don't think they'll just gun me down. They do that and the sheriff'll have to do *something*."

"Maybe that's what we've got to do," Clint said.

"What?"

"Somehow force the sheriff into taking some kind of action."

"And how do we do that?"

Clint looked at Charlie, eased his weight over to his good side and said, "I don't know yet.

TWENTY-FIVE

Sheriff Paxton looked up as his office door opened, and he frowned. He didn't know the man who had entered.

"Can I help you?" he asked.

Virtue took the time to look around the office. The two deputies he'd seen outside the cantina the night before were nowhere to be seen. He turned his attention back to the sheriff.

"My name's Del Virtue," he said. "That mean anything to you?"

Paxton frowned, thought a moment. "I can't say it does. Should I know you?"

"Yeah, you should," Virtue said, annoyed.

"What's your business, Mr. Virtue?"

Virtue decided to push right away and find out if the man had any bottom to him.

"My business is whatever I make it, Sheriff," Virtue said. "Right now there are two men in town who are my business."

"Oh? Who would that be?"

"You saw them last night," Virtue said. "Seems they killed five of your townsmen."

"They were bandidos, not from town," the lawman said.

"Not my point," Virtue said. "You know the two men I'm talkin' about?"

"Clint Adams is one of them."

"Right, the Gunsmith," Virtue said. "I plan to make him my business. I need to know if I can count on you."

Paxton started to get a bad feeling. He swallowed before answering.

"Count on me for what?"

Virtue perched a hip on the sheriff's desk and stared down at the man. Looking into the man's eyes, he saw just what he wanted to see, that the sheriff was not going to be any trouble at all.

"To stay out of my way, star packer," Virtue said. "I've got some men with me and I need you and your deputies to leave us to what we're gonna do."

Paxton opened his mouth to ask a question and nothing came out. He swallowed and tried again.

"W-what is that gonna be?"

"You'll find out after the fact," Virtue said, standing up. "Take my advice and stay clear of that part of town for a while."

"W-when . . . when is all this gonna happen?"

"I don't know," Virtue said. "Next couple of days, probably. Just steer clear, Sheriff. In fact, I'll even let you know when we're leavin' town. How's that?"

"That's . . . that's . . . that'll be . . . fine."

"Good," Virtue said. "I knew I'd get cooperation from you, Sheriff."

Paxton didn't say anything.

Virtue started for the door, then stopped and turned back.

"Oh, me and my men are in one of your hotels, and we'll be drinkin' and eatin' around town. There's about seven of us. Ask your deputies to give us a wide berth, understand?"

"I-I understand."

"Good," Virtue said. He gave the lawman one last hard look, then opened the door and left.

Paxton took a deep breath, dug a bottle of whiskey out of his bottom drawer and drank straight from it. He knew one of the livery stables in town was for sale. It was time for him to change occupations.

Charlie came back to Clint's room after checking the front and the back of the building.

"We've got two men watching," he said. "One out front and one in the back."

"Know them?"

"Never saw 'em before."

Clint turned his eyes toward the boarded up window.

"That's what I was thinkin'," Charlie said. "I got to go out a window, pick one that neither one of them can see."

"Check in with the sheriff, see what he knows."

"Then I can come walkin' back in the front door and surprise 'em," Charlie said.

"You sure you want to taunt them that way?"

"Oh, yeah," Charlie said. "Why not?"

"Up to you," Clint said. "You want to use this window?"

"I thought the room next door," Charlie said. "I can open it and close it myself."

"Okay," Clint said. "Just check in with the law, see what you can find out and come back. I'd say try not to run into anybody, but since we don't know what they look like . . ."

"Except for these two," he said. "If they're different from the two who were creepin' around last night, that would make four."

"Good," Clint said, "let's figure four, at least. And the presence of these two means we're not overreacting."

"No," Charlie said, agreeing, "it's pretty clear now that somebody's out to get us."

"Or me," Clint said. "Somebody's out to get me."

"You, me," Charlie said, "same thing."

Charlie walked across the room, got Clint's rifle and handed it to him. Clint already had his modified Colt hanging in its holster on the bedpost, so he accepted the rifle.

"Keep that handy until I get back."

"I'll keep it close to heart," Clint said. "You be careful."

"Always."

As Charlie Utter left the room, Clint thought that he'd never seen the man look so happy.

TWENTY-SIX

Charlie Utter opened the window slowly, slipped out as
quietly as he could and then closed the window behind
him. He looked both ways and was satisfied that nobody
was watching him. Now he had to get out of this alley
without either of the men seeing him. Luckily, the building
next to the cantina and hotel did not extend as far back,
and he was able to go around it and make his way to the
front street. From that vantage point he could see the man
who was watching the front of the building. He was going
to have to go the other way, down the street rather than up
the street, and circle around that man to get to the sheriff's
office.

They were going to be shocked when he came walking
back later . . .

Sheriff Paxton had not yet recovered from Del Virtue's
visit—the man had been scary!—when the door to his office opened and Charlie Utter entered.

"What the hell—" Paxton said, then saw it was Charlie
and not Virtue again.

"We need to talk, Sheriff," Charlie said.

"I've done enough talkin' for one day, Utter," Paxton said.

"Not to me, you haven't," Charlie said. "I need some information from you."

"What makes you think I can help you?"

"Because you're the law," Charlie said.

"Is that right?" Paxton shocked Charlie by taking off his badge and dropping it on the desk. "Not anymore."

"What are you doin'?" Charlie asked, suspicious.

"Resignin'."

"Why?"

"Because you and Adams brought trouble with you to El Paso, Utter, trouble I don't want nothin' to do with." He stood up. "This ain't my job or my office no more."

"What about your deputies?"

"Let one of them take over if they want."

Paxton started around the desk, his intent to leave, but Charlie pushed him back.

"What th—"

"Sheriff or no sheriff," he said, "you got the information I need, don't ya?"

"I don't know what you mean."

Charlie drew his gun, but didn't point it at the man. He just held it down at his side.

"Well then, ain't neither one of us is leavin' this office until you do," he said.

The man watching the front of the cantina was Pitt, while Thorpe watched the back. When a man came walking down the street, right up to the front door of the cantina, and used a key to let himself in, Pitt didn't know what to do. He didn't know who the man was. He could have been the proper owner, for all Pitt knew. Once the man went inside, Pitt decided to go find Thorpe and ask him what they should do.

• • •

When Charlie entered Clint's room, he found himself looking down the barrel of a rifle.

"It's just me."

Clint put up the rifle and said, "Well, knock next time."

"I got a present for ya."

He tossed something shiny onto the bed. Clint picked it up and saw that it was a sheriff's badge.

"Where did you get this?"

"From Sheriff Paxton," Charlie said, then added, "I mean, ex-Sheriff Paxton."

"Ex?"

"He decided to resign rather than deal with what he said was more trouble than he wanted to handle."

"Did you find out what we need to know?"

"Yeah," Charlie said, "he wasn't real anxious to talk, but I persuaded him to."

"And?"

"We're lookin' at seven men led by a fella named Virtue, Del Virtue," Charlie said. "You ever heard of him?"

"Yeah," Clint said, "I'm afraid I have, but only because he was the man in Magdalena who had me holed up in the hotel, only he had four men with him then, not six."

"Guess he picked up a couple more guns to take care of me."

"And I guess he scared the shit out of the sheriff, huh?" Clint asked.

"Oh, yeah . . ."

Clint looked at the tin star in his hand.

"So why did we end up with this?"

"I don't know," Charlie said. "A souvenir, maybe? Or maybe we can get some use out of it?"

Clint tossed it back to Charlie.

"You hang onto it. Maybe you'll have to wear it to justify what we have to do."

"I ain't exactly been sworn in."

Clint shrugged. "Who's going to know for sure?"

"You want me to pretend to be the sheriff?"

"No," Clint said, "I want you to put it on and be the sheriff.

TWENTY-SEVEN

"You did what?" Del Virtue asked.

Thorpe and Pitt looked at each other, and then at Steve Nash.

"You let him walk out, and then back in again?" Nash asked.

"Well," Pitt said, "we never saw him walk out, so when he walked in we didn't know who he was."

"I was in the back," Thorpe said. "I didn't see a thing."

Pitt gave a look that said, "Thanks a lot for the backup."

"What did he look like?" Virtue asked.

"Not much," Pitt said, "short, with yellow hair—"

"That was Utter."

They were in the cantina that Virtue seemed to have picked out for a base of operations. The four of them were seated at a table while the rest of the men were at the bar. The bartender had a look of misery on his face, because ever since the gringos took over he had no business. And these men were not paying for their drinks. Jones and Horrigan were smirking as the two new men squirmed.

"I thought you said these boys were good boys," Virtue said to Nash. "You vouched for them, Nash."

"Yeah, I did," Nash said, "but—"

"Never mind," Virtue said. "Let's assume that Charlie Utter got out of the hotel and then walked back in. What does he know now that he didn't know before?"

"Who we are?" Nash asked. "And how many?"

"And who woulda told him that?"

The table was silent and then Nash asked, "The sheriff?"

"I wouldn't have thought so," Virtue said, "not after our talk, but I guess we'd better go and find out."

He and Nash stood up, followed by Thorpe and Pitt.

"Not you two," Virtue said. "Stay right here and wait for us. Have a drink. Have two drinks."

"We still got jobs, Mr. Virtue?" Pitt asked.

"Can you still use a gun?"

"Yes, sir."

"Then you still got jobs," Virtue said, "only because I need guns."

"What about us, Del?" Neal Jones asked from the bar.

"Just wait here. We'll be back."

Charlie came back from checking both the front and the back. "Our watchers are gone."

"They probably know I've been shot and can't ride."

"We could still get out of this building while nobody's watchin'," Charlie said.

"And go where? I can't walk any better than I can ride. No, we'd better stay here. We're better off here than out in the open."

"What's this Virtue got against you, anyway?"

"What did any man want of Bill when they came to try him, Charlie?" Clint asked.

"But this . . . this ain't callin' you out into the street for a fair fight. I mean . . . five against one in Magdalena, seven against two here? If they end up killin' us that's . . . well, that's murder."

"That won't be the way they tell it," Clint said. "All

they'll claim is that they killed the Gunsmith. That's all they want."

"You know," Charlie said, "if there's a telegraph office in town, I could send for help."

"We could do that," Clint said. "I'm sure we've both got friends around the country, but how long would it take them to get here? This thing would come to a head way before that."

"What if we make a deal with Virtue and his men?" Charlie asked, still thinking.

"What kind of a deal?"

"If they'll wait until you're healed, we'll face them."

"On the street?" Clint asked. "Seven against two?"

"You don't think we could take 'em?"

Clint had to think a minute. If they were standing with Bat Masterson, or Wyatt Earp, or Bill Hickok, maybe. But him and Charlie Utter? There was nothing in Charlie's past to suggest that he was a fast gun, or that he was very accurate. Mostly he had a past as a loyal friend to Hickok.

"I don't know, Charlie," Clint said. "I think maybe we ought to save that for later, as a last resort."

"Sure," Charlie said. "I understand. You hungry?"

"Charlie—" Clint wanted to say something to the man to assure him that it wasn't that he didn't have faith in him.

"Naw, that's okay, Clint," Charlie said, cutting him off. "I'm gonna go and rustle up some grub."

As the man left, Clint realized he couldn't go out on the street and face seven guns just to make Charlie Utter feel better. He didn't think either of them would want that.

Del Virtue sat behind the sheriff's desk, waiting. They had found the office empty, and he had sent Steve Nash out to try and find the lawman. When the door opened, a man wearing a badge came stumbling in, but he wasn't the sheriff. He was a deputy.

"Found this one on the street, Del."

Virtue was surprised. Coming back with a deputy showed initiative on Nash's part. He wasn't used to that.

"What's your name?"

"K-Kenny," the young man said.

"Deputy Kenny?"

"Kenny Mills," the deputy said.

"Well, Deputy Kenny Mills, where's your boss?"

"I dunno," Mills said. "I been lookin' for him myself."

"For how long?"

"Coupla hours."

Virtue wondered if he had scared the man enough to make him leave town.

"Is your boss a brave man, Deputy Kenny?"

"No, sir," the young man said, "not at all."

"How about you?" Virtue asked. "You brave?"

"Not really."

"Then why are you wearin' a badge?"

The young man shrugged. "It's a job."

"A job, huh?" Virtue asked. "I saw another deputy the other night. Who's he?"

"That was Jeb," Mills said. "He's just p-part time."

"So you're the only full-time deputy?"

"Yes, sir."

"Well," Virtue said, "I tell you what, Deputy Kenny. You're plumb out of a job."

"W-what?"

"You're fired," Virtue said.

"B-but—"

"You wanna be a brave man now, son?"

Mills looked over his shoulder at Nash, who was smiling, and then back at Virtue.

"No, sir."

"Then unpin that badge, drop it on the desk and go with God, boy," Virtue said. "I'm doin' you a favor and savin' your life."

"Y-yes, sir."

Mills took the badge off, stepped up to the desk and dropped it on top.

"T-thank you, si—"

"Get out!" Virtue shouted.

Ex-Deputy Kenny Mills turned and ran for the door.

"Wait a minute!"

Mills froze.

"Steve, take that boy's gun. We don't want him hurtin' himself."

"Sure, Del."

Nash approached the deputy and removed his gun from his holster.

"Okay, boy," he said, "git!"

Mills opened the door and ran out.

"Looks like there's no law left in El Paso, Steve," Virtue said. "Whataya think of that?"

TWENTY-EIGHT

Charlie thought about pinning the sheriff's badge on, but since he wasn't really the law, he decided just to put it in his shirt pocket.

Clint decided to leave the door to his room open, since in effect the entire place was theirs. Some sunlight filtered in through the wooden slats on the window, so he knew it was dusk when they disappeared.

Charlie kept on the move, as if patrolling the entire building. Clint would see him go by his door, then up and down the hall. Occasionally he'd stop in with a cup of coffee, or a beer. Clint wasn't drinking whiskey anymore. He'd only needed it that first night to get to sleep, while his wound was fresh.

A few times during the day he decided to try and walk himself. Each time he'd push himself too far and have to lean on Charlie to get back, but he thought he was getting better, stronger. He was determined to whittle the doctor's prediction of weeks down to days. If Del Virtue and his men didn't come for them in the next few days, maybe they'd be able to get out of El Paso and into the open expanse of Mexico. They'd have a much better chance against seven men out in the open, rather than in this build-ing or out in the street.

"Think they'll come for us at night?" Charlie asked, leaning against the doorway.

"I think they're going to want it to look as legitimate as possible," Clint said, "and that means broad daylight. Coming for us at night would be a last resort, I think."

"I'll stay on watch, anyway."

"When's the last time you slept, Charlie?" Clint asked.

"Can't say I remember."

"I think it's time you got some sleep," Clint said. "I'll take the first watch."

"Are you sure you're up to it?"

"I just have to stay awake and alert for four hours, then wake you," Clint said. "What's so hard?"

"Where do you want to do it?"

"In the hall would be good," Clint said. "That way I can cover the front and back."

"Can you sit in a chair?"

"If we pad it with pillows. Also, take that bead curtain down from the front entrance so I can see right into the cantina."

"Right."

Charlie got things arranged for Clint, then went into one of the rooms to get some sleep.

"Remember," he said, "wake me in four hours. You're in no shape to stay up all night."

"Don't worry," Clint said, "I'm not going to take the chance of falling asleep and getting us both killed."

"Okay," Charlie said, yawning. "Truth is I could use a few hours."

"You got 'em, pard," Clint said.

The truth was Clint could not get comfortable on the wooden chair, even with a couple of pillows as padding. Also, he continued to worry about the horses—Eclipse, in particular. The Darley Arabian meant a lot to him, and he was concerned that Virtue and his gang might hurt him. Maybe in the morning Charlie would be able to sneak out and bring the horses back here. They sure had enough room to keep them inside.

Clint tried walking up and down the hall a bit, careful not to go too far since Charlie was asleep and would not be able to help him. He'd taken the bullet in the left hip, and while the doc said it wasn't serious it did rob his left leg of some strength.

Halfway through his watch he got hungry, but he didn't think he'd be able to make it to the kitchen and back. He should have had Charlie leave something with him.

Finally, in the last hour, he was able to sit in the chair and relax a bit. He toyed with the idea of giving Charlie an extra hour or two, but he was fading and it'd be too dangerous. If he fell asleep, they could be overrun before he knew it.

He fought like hell to keep awake that last hour and finally woke Charlie on time.

Del Virtue had decided to forsake the cantina as a base of operations and just use the sheriff's office.

Nash was nosing around the office and said, "If that lawman ran out, he took the badge with him."

"What if he didn't run out after I talked to him?" Virtue asked.

"Then when?"

"What if Utter got out of the hotel—maybe through a window—and came here to talk to the sheriff?"

"About what?"

"It would help him and Adams to know who we are, how many we are."

"And the sheriff knew that?"

Yes, damnit, Virtue thought, thanks to me. He had not only told the sheriff his name, but how many men he had.

"He might have."

"Del, why don't we just go in tonight and take them?" Nash asked.

"We got time, Steve," Virtue said. "There's no law here, no hurry. That little building is solid, like a fortress. I just need some time to figure out a way to get them to come out."

"We could set it on fire," Nash said.

"We could," Virtue said, "but it's an adobe building. Everything inside would burn, but probably not the structure."

"The smoke would drive them out."

"Yeah, it might," Virtue said, wondering when Nash had decided to start thinking. "I'll just take a little longer to try and figure it out, if you don't mind."

"You're the boss, Del."

At least Nash always remembered that.

TWENTY-NINE

Clint woke to rays of light streaming in between the slats on the window. They were thin beams, though, because Charlie had been careful not to leave enough space for a gun barrel to poke though.

Clint rolled into a sitting position and flinched. His hip had stiffened during the night. It would take a walk from here to the kitchen to loosen it up. He stood, retrieved his gunbelt from the bedpost, slung it over his shoulder and left the room. As with the morning before, he could smell Charlie Utter cooking in the kitchen.

Breakfast was the same, this time with some extra tortillas to soak up the meat and beans and eggs.

"We got enough food to stay in here a week," Charlie said.

"Any guns or ammo?"

"An old Greener behind the bar and some shells," Charlie said. "And a Navy Colt in the storeroom that might blow up in your hand if you ever tried to fire it."

"Well," Clint said, "I guess we have enough ammo for a fight, but not for a siege."

"The question is, when do we fight?"

"And do we even have the choice?" Clint asked. "I think that might be up to Virtue and his men."

"Is there any way we can take that decision away from them?"

"We can walk out the front door," Clint said. "That would trigger a fight almost immediately."

"We can't do that right now," Charlie said. "Doc says you need a few weeks."

"I'll be ready in a few days," Clint assured him. "The question becomes, do we have a few days?"

Charlie rubbed his forehead, as if he had a headache.

"You go through this a lot?" he asked.

"About as much as Bill did, I imagine."

"Not really," Charlie said. "Bill had somethin' you don't seem to have, Clint."

"What's that?"

"People were afraid of him. I mean, not just his reputation, but him. When he walked in a room, they all stared at him but nobody thought about tryin' him. They were too scared."

"You telling me I've got to be scarier?"

"I'm just sayin' you probably have gone through this kind of thing a lot more than Bill," Charlie said. "I don't see how you can stand it."

"I don't have much choice," Clint said. "Unless I go into hiding, it's going to happen a lot more."

"Until . . . what?"

"Until somebody finally beats me, puts me down," Clint said, "or shoots me from behind like they did Bill."

Charlie shook his head.

"Like I said, I don't know how you stand it."

Virtue woke with a naked woman next to him. Steve Nash had found the whorehouse when he got to town and had tried it. He assured Virtue that the woman in his bed was a good one.

Well, she'd proven the point the night before. She was very skilled and had been able to stay with him no matter how rough he got.

The woman rolled over onto her back, her big breasts flattening out. Virtue didn't mind that. He liked extra meat on his women. She was the older whore who had flim-flammed Nash that first day. She'd already found Virtue to be smarter than Nash, so she hadn't tried to fool him at all. She just gave him what he wanted, hard fast sex, a suck job later. After that they'd both gone to sleep, and she appreciated that fact. It was the most sleep she'd had in some time.

"Wake up," Virtue said, reaching out and grabbing one big breast.

"Hmm?" She opened her eyes, looked at him and stretched. Her black hair was a wild black cloud fanned out on the pillow. Her nipples were large, dark brown, and as he thumbed one it tightened and came awake. "You are ready for more, gringo?"

"I need you to wake me up, Angel," he said, remembering her name. It was actually Angelique, but she used Angel.

She rolled over on top of him and reached down between his legs. His penis was very large, even when flaccid. She was impressed when she first saw it, and even more so when she discovered that he knew how to use it. He did not just lie there and make her do all the work.

As she rubbed him, he grew in her hand. She dangled her breasts in his face so he could suck her nipples, and his hands came around to cup her big buttocks.

"Mmm," she said, "you are ready."

"Oh, yeah," he said, "I'm ready."

And she was, too. Her pussy was so wet he slid right into her, all the way to the hilt, and she gasped, closed her eyes and smiled.

"*Aye, dios,*" she said. "You fill me up, *vato.*"

"I'm gonna do more than that, Angel," he promised. He flipped her over so that he was on top, then began to fuck her, slowly at first, and then faster. She lifted her knees up to open herself even more, then raked his back with her nails. He didn't seem to mind the pain, and she actually liked inflicting it.

This one, she thought, even though he is a gringo, was a good match for her.

THIRTY

Charlie cleaned up after breakfast, and they remained at the table sharing another pot of coffee and talking about the horses.

"I guess I could try to get out and bring them back here," Charlie said. "Don't know that I could do it without attracting attention."

"It would help to have them here," Clint said. "For one thing, we could stop worrying about them."

"Well," Charlie said, "I can see why you're worried about yours. I'm not that worried about mine. It's just a horse."

"That's true," Clint said. "But I don't want anything to happen to Eclipse."

"I never name my animals," Charlie said. "I never wanted to name somethin' I might hafta eat."

"Are we being watched today?"

"There's a man on the front," Charlie said, "but not on the back. I guess I could leave that way and try to get back here with the horses the same way."

"Somebody would notice," Clint said. "What we need is some kind of diversion."

"Like what?"

"I don't know yet," Clint said. "But let's think of something."

The man Virtue had put out front to watch the building was Neal Jones, who he felt he could count on more than any of the others, after Steve Nash.

"They're not gonna sneak out the back," Virtue said. "Not with that bullet wound in Adams's hip."

"I'll stand watch," Jones said, "but if they slip out the back and go for their horses—"

"Don't worry about that. Just stand watch."

Jones found himself a chair and set himself up in front of the hardware store. The one thing he didn't like about working for Del Virtue was that the man had to look at every damn angle before he made a decision. He settled in for a long day.

After Virtue had sent Jones to stand watch, he pulled Ben Horrigan aside. "Find their horses," he told him.

"They could be anywhere."

"There can't be more than a few livery stables in town," Virtue told him. "Just look in all of them."

"How am I supposed to know which horses are theirs?"

"I'm not worried about Utter's horse," Virtue said, "but Adams thinks a lot of that big black he has. Find that one."

"Okay," Horrigan said, "I'll go out and find a big black horse. What're you gonna be doin'?"

Virtue just stared at the man until he left. Virtue sat back in the sheriff's chair. He liked this office. Maybe he'd stay on in El Paso afterward as the sheriff—a sheriff with a big rep for killing the Gunsmith.

"This sounds dangerous," Charlie told Clint.

"All I'm going to do is sit in the front window, where they can see me," Clint said.

"Or take a shot at you."

"They'd have to hit me with the first one."

"Oh, sure, at the first sound of a shot you're gonna hit the deck? With that hip? You'll be lucky if you can move."

"Look, Charlie," Clint said, "this is the only plan I could come up with. You come up with something else."

Charlie couldn't.

"Besides," Clint added, "you've got the dangerous part. Get back here with the horses."

"They might have somebody watchin' the horses," Charlie said. "I'll have to kill him."

"If you do," Clint said, "that'll be one less gun we'll have to worry about."

They set up a table and chairs near the front window of the cantina, and pulled back the curtains that partially hid the window. Then Clint sat himself down there with his gun.

"I still don't like this," Charlie said.

"There's been no shot yet," Clint said, "and look, he's already seen me."

They looked across the street. The man on watch had sat forward in his chair and was staring across the street.

"Yeah, you got his attention," Charlie said.

"You'd better get going," Clint said. "Get back here as fast as you can."

"I'll do my best."

Neal Jones was startled to see Clint Adams sitting in the window of the cantina. He sat forward in his chair and peered across the street, trying to be sure. He had seen Adams in Magdalena, was pretty sure he'd know him on sight. Yeah, after a few moments of staring, he was sure it was Adams.

Now what was he supposed to do? Keep watching or go and tell Virtue that he'd seen the Gunsmith. Adams wasn't doing anything, he was just sitting there. Jones guessed that wasn't much to report on. He decided to wait until he saw some definite activity.

So he sat back in his chair again, chewed on a toothpick and kept his eyes on Clint Adams.

THIRTY-ONE

Charlie successfully slipped out the back door. He'd left his rifle behind so he wouldn't have to carry anything. He figured he'd need both hands to lead the two horses.

This was easier than sneaking out the window. He was able to move around behind the hotel without danger of being seen. If it had been him, he would have put a man on the back, but there was no accounting for the decisions some people made.

The livery was several blocks away and he started to make his way over there, without using the main street.

Ben Horrigan didn't know where the livery stables were, so he wandered around town trying to find them. In the first one he found a bunch of swaybacked horses with no sign of the Gunsmith's big black. When he got to the second livery stable, he found a better class of horse and was about to leave when he suddenly saw something in a back stall. It was an animal that seemed to tower above all the others. It was larger and in another class.

It was a big black gelding the likes of nothing he'd ever seen before. He'd heard people talk about the Gun-

smith's horse, but had never seen it, not even in Magdalena.

He was damn sure he'd found what he was looking for.

Charlie got to the livery just as a man wearing a gun was
walking in. He had no horse, so he was either picking one
up . . . or he was looking for something. He peered inside,
saw the man checking stalls, then watched as he went to
the stall that held Clint's Darley Arabian. The man looked
very happy.

At that moment the Mexican who owned the livery
came in the back door and saw the gunman, who also saw
him.

"Hey, senor," the gunman said. "Who's horse is this?"

The liveryman looked at the other man, frowning.

"*El horso*," the gunman said. "Belongs to who?" he
pointed at the big black.

Finally the man got the idea, but he just shrugged and
said, "Gringo."

"Yeah, gringo," the man said. "That's what I thought."

Charlie watched and waited. If the gunman tried to take
the horse, he was going to have to stop him. If, on the other
hand, he was happy just to have located the animal, and he
left, Charlie could still grab the horse.

He waited, keeping his fingers crossed.

Horrigan had two choices. Take the animal with him, or
just go and tell Virtue that he found it. To take it with him,
he was going to have to get past this liveryman. He was
sure he could, but he knew that Virtue didn't want him to
cause any trouble while they were in town. Not until they
were ready to move. Besides, where would he put the
horse?

He decided to leave it where it was.

•   •   •

Charlie withdrew as the gunman started for the front entrance of the livery. He watched the man leave and head back toward town. He was probably going to report to his boss.

Charlie didn't know how long he had, so he ducked right into the livery.

"*Buenos dios,*" the liveryman said, with a bow.

"You remember me?" Charlie asked.

"*Sí,*" the man said. "*Dos caballos.*"

"That's right," Charlie said. The liveryman held up two fingers. "Two horses. I'm gonna take them now. How much? *Cuanto?*"

Charlie took out some money and gave it to the man, who seemed to be insisting that it was too much.

"That's okay," Charlie said. "That's okay. I've got to get them saddled."

For some reason the liveryman saddled his horse while Charlie warily saddled Clint's. The big animal surprised him and stood still while he did it. When the two horses were saddled, Charlie took the reins of both and said to the liveryman, "*Gracias.*"

"*Por nada, señor. Vaya con dios.*"

It was as if the man knew they were in trouble and wanted to help them get away.

"Well, where is it?" Virtue asked Horrigan.

"Uh, it's in the stable."

"You found the Gunsmith's horse and you left it there?"

"Uh, you didn't tell me—"

Virtue got up from the sheriff's desk and said, "Come on, goddamnit. Show me!"

Charlie led both horses along alleys and behind buildings. He was able to get back to the hotel without going on the main street. When he reached the rear of the cantina, he opened the door and led both horses inside.

• • •

Clint heard the noise from his table and was able to crane his neck and peer down the hall. The first thing he saw was Charlie leading both horses inside.

"By God," he said, "you got them."

THIRTY-TWO

Del Virtue stared at the empty stall, then looked at Ben Horrigan.

"Where is it?" he asked. "Did it just wander out of here by itself?"

"I don't know, Del," Horrigan said. "I swear it was there twenty minutes ago."

"Find the liveryman and see if somebody came and got the horse," Virtue said. "And see if another horse was taken, too. I'm gonna go and see what Neal saw."

"But . . . the guy doesn't speak English," Horrigan called out as Del Virtue left.

"Figure it out!"

When Clint Adams moved out of the window, Neal Jones was in the same predicament he'd been in when he first saw Adams. Go and tell Virtue, or wait. He didn't have to think about it for very long, though, because the very next moment Del Virtue appeared at his elbow.

"What's goin' on?" he asked.

"Well . . . Adams has been sitting in that window for the past hour or so," Jones said.

"Doin' what?"

Jones shrugged. "Just sittin'."

"Where? I don't see him."

"He just got up and left."

Virtue stared at the cantina and came to a decision.

"Go get the others," he said. "I'm goin' across the street."

"Del—"

"Just do it!" Virtue snapped.

Clint and Charlie picked out a room and put both horses in it. As if to claim the space for their own, both animals lifted their tails and made a deposit on the floor.

"Okay," Clint said, "they're comfortable."

"I should have brought some feed," Charlie said, as they left the room.

"Check the storeroom for something we can give them," Clint said. "If there's nothing, at least we can let them have water. Hopefully, we won't all be cooped up here much longer."

Virtue went around behind the building and saw the fresh tracks of horses in the dirt. Satisfied that Clint Adams and Charlie Utter had somehow gotten their horses into the hotel, Virtue felt he had only one play.

He went back around to the front of the hotel and banged on the front door.

"What the hell—" Charlie said at the sound of banging.

"Somebody wants in," Clint said, "or wants to talk."

"Do we wanna to talk to them?" Charlie asked.

"Why not?" Clint said. "Maybe we can settle this before somebody else gets killed."

"I'll get it—"

"Wait," Clint said, "I'll come, too."

They got Clint situated at a table—not the one by the window—and then Charlie went to answer the door.

"Whataya want?" he asked.

"My name is Del Virtue," the man answered. "I want to talk to the Gunsmith."

"Maybe he don't wanna talk to you," Charlie said.

"You're Colorado Charlie Utter," Virtue said.

"That's right."

"Well, I think you're wrong, Charlie," Virtue said. "I think Adams does wanna talk to me."

Charlie hesitated a moment, then said, "Come on in."

"Do you want my gun?"

"If I asked you for it, would you give up?"

Virtue chuckled and said. "No."

"Then come on in," Charlie said, again. "You're out-gunned, so I don't think you'll try anythin'."

As Virtue entered, Charlie looked outside. Across the street it looked like his men were gathering.

"You got friends across the street," he said, closing the door.

"They won't do anything."

"Why not?"

"They have no orders," Virtue said, "and they ain't smart enough to make a decision on their own. They'll wait."

"Doesn't sound like a particularly good bunch to have," Clint said, from his table.

"You'd be surprised," Virtue said. "I always find the best gang to have is one that waits for orders."

"I prefer men who can think, myself."

"Hello, Adams."

"Virtue."

"I've tracked you a long way."

"Well," Clint said, "why don't we have Charlie get us some beers and we can talk about it."

THIRTY-THREE

When they all had a beer, Virtue sat down opposite Clint at the table. Charlie remained at the bar. From that vantage point he could see Virtue and the men across the street.

"Heard you took a bullet in the hip."

"It's not bad."

"Got shot by a little girl."

Clint smiled.

"Little girl," he said, "big gun."

"Look," Virtue said, "I tracked you all the way here from Magdalena. We could have done this there, but you decided to go out a back window."

"Five-against-one odds didn't sit well with me that day, Mr. Virtue," Clint said.

"Hey, you can call me Del," Virtue said. "I always like to be on a first name basis with a man I'm gonna kill . . . Clint."

"I tell you what I'll do, Del," Clint said. "Even with this bullet in my hip I'll face you in the street. Just you and me. Your men stay out of it, Charlie stays out of it. Only one person dies—you or me."

"You know, I would take that offer in a minute, Clint,"

Virtue said, "if I thought I had a chance in hell of beatin' you . . . but I don't."

"So you intend to kill me . . . how? By gunnin' me down in the street, seven guns blazing? How's that going to look as a reputation, Del?"

"All anyone will ever remember is that I was the man who killed you," Virtue said. "Nobody's gonna remember how."

"You're wrong about that," Charlie said from behind Virtue.

"Ah, our friend Mr. Utter's got somethin' to say."

"Everybody remembers how a man with a reputation is killed," Charlie said. "Everybody remembers that Wild Bill Hickok was killed by a coward. Everybody remembers Jesse James was killed by a coward. If you manage to kill Clint, you'll be remembered the same way—as a coward."

"Now you, Charlie," Virtue said, "I would face in the street."

"Anytime," Charlie said, "just you and me, winner takes all."

"No, that ain't what I meant," Virtue said. "I meant, after we kill ol' Clint, here."

"So we're back where we started," Clint said. "You'd like me to step out into the street to face you and six men. It is six now, isn't it? Four in Magdalena, but six here?"

"Well," Virtue said, "you picked up some help along the way, too."

"What about the law in El Paso?" Clint asked.

"There ain't any," Virtue said. "The sheriff's disappeared, and his deputies have resigned. In fact, I've taken over his office, but I can't find his badge."

"You mean this one?" Charlie took it out of his pocket and tossed it. It landed on the table between Clint and Virtue. Clint wondered if Charlie meant for that to happen.

"So you did talk to him."

"Right after you did," Charlie said.

"I think you both scared him out of town," Clint said.

"So you got his badge, I got his office," Virtue said.

"What good does his office do you?" Clint asked.

"What good's his badge if you ain't been sworn in?"

"Your men are gettin' restless," Charlie said, watching them mill around across the street.

"They come charging in here," Clint added, "you know you're going to get the first bullet."

"Like I tol' you," Virtue said, "they won't do a thing unless they hear from me."

"And if they don't?" Charlie asked.

"What?"

"If they don't hear from you, what will they do?"

"Why would they not—"

Virtue stopped when he heard the cocking of the hammer on Charlie's gun, and then felt the gun barrel against the back of his head.

"I'm sayin'," Charlie went on, "if you never walk out of here, what will they do?"

"Just a guess," Virtue said, "but I guess they'd leave. You fellas would be in the clear."

Virtue looked across the table and smiled.

"I hear that Colorado Charlie here was real upset about his friend Hickok gettin' shot in the back of the head," he said. "Is he gonna do the same to me, now?"

"Charlie . . ." Clint said.

"It sure would make things simple, wouldn't it, Clint?" Charlie asked.

"Yeah, it would," Clint said, "but you wouldn't be able to live with yourself after."

"We could turn him around and shoot him in the front," Charlie said. "I could live with that."

"I couldn't," Clint said. "Besides, there's no guarantee his men would leave town."

"I'll give you boys until the end of the day," Virtue said. "Step out and shoot it out like men. Otherwise, tomorrow mornin', we're comin' in."

Virtue stood up and stepped away from the table and from Charlie's gun. He walked to the door, opened it and then looked at Clint.

"If I was you, I woulda let him kill me."

"That's the difference between you and me, Del," Clint said.

Virtue shrugged and left.

THIRTY-FOUR

"I shoulda killed him," Charlie said. "One of us shoulda killed him."

"You're probably right."

Clint shifted his weight, winced. His bandage had become tacky, it felt as if his wound were being pulled apart.

"You in pain?"

"This bandage needs to be changed."

"And the wound needs to be cleaned," Charlie said. "Can you make it back to your room? I'll get some water and bandages."

"Check out front first," Clint said.

Charlie went to the window and looked out.

"There's only one man across the street again."

"And they probably put one in the back," Clint said. "Okay, I can make my way to my room."

He got up and walked down the hall to his room. The smell of horseshit was unmistakable, and he knew that Del Virtue had been able to smell it, as well. He also knew that Charlie was right. Killing Virtue probably would have ended everything, but he was too damn moral for a man with a reputation. He'd been told that before, and it was true.

He was on the bed when Charlie appeared with a basin of water and some bandages.

"Get them pants off," Charlie said, "and let's get ta work . . ."

When Virtue joined his men across the street, he said, "Thorpe, you take the back. Pitt, the front. If either of you see anybody leavin' that buildin', start shootin'. We'll hear it and come runnin'. Ya got it?"

"We got it," Thorpe said.

"The rest of you come with me to the sheriff's office."

Connors, Horrigan, Neal Jones and Steve Nash all followed him to the sheriff's office.

"What happened in there?" Jones asked when they were inside.

"I told them they had until mornin' to come out," Virtue said.

"Then shouldn't we be over there, waitin' for them?" Horrigan asked.

"No," Virtue said, "they ain't comin' out. They don't like the odds."

"We heard they got their horses," Nash said.

"Yeah," Connors added, "what happens if they come ridin' out?"

"Adams can't sit a horse, yet," Virtue said. "Naw, they'll wait until mornin' to see what we're gonna do."

"And what are we gonna do?" Jones asked.

"Can't say I got that figured out exactly yet," Virtue said, "but I'll tell you one thing."

"What's that?"

"By this time tomorrow, the Gunsmith's gonna be dead."

Charlie cleaned Clint's wound good, rebandaged it, then helped him get seated on the bed.

"All that movin' around made you start to bleed again," he said. "You better stay still for a while."

"For the night, anyway," Clint said.

"Ain't no way you're gonna be able to ride, Clint."

"I could probably manage a short ride, if we stopped soon," Clint said, "but that wouldn't be the case. They'd be after us."

"Soon as we broke through that front door," Charlie said. "I see we been thinkin' the same thing."

"It would work for you, Charlie," Clint said, "not for me. You could break through and ride hell bent for leather. They'd never catch you."

"I already told ya I ain't gonna leave ya, Clint," Charlie said, "so that ain't a good plan."

"Okay, okay," Clint said, "be stubborn."

"Anyway," Charlie said, "we got the night to worry about it. Why don't you get some rest and I'll wake you up later for some grub."

"Sounds good."

"I gotta give that bastard credit," Charlie said.

"Who?"

"Virtue," Charlie said. "He come walkin' in like that, it took balls."

"Yeah, it did," Clint said, lying on his side.

"I don't know how he figured we wouldn't just kill 'im."

"Because it was something he would do," Clint said, "he figured we wouldn't."

"I was close," Charlie said. "Real close."

Clint peered over his shoulder at Charlie.

"I don't think you were that close, Charlie," he said. "Not in the back of the head, anyway. Not after what happened to Bill."

Charlie hung his head a moment, then looked at Clint.

"You're probably right," he finally said. "Get some rest. I'll see you later."

"Sure."

•   •   •

Charlie went back to the kitchen, wondering what Bill
Hickok would have done in Clint's place. Would he have let
Virtue walk out of the cantina alive? No, Bill probably
would've killed him, then went outside with both of his guns
to face the other six, and whatever happened happened.

But that would have been Hickok's move and not the
smart move. Toward the end of his life Charlie kind of
thought Bill was looking for death.

Clint Adams wasn't at that point in his life, and Charlie
didn't think he ever would be.

THIRTY-FIVE

Virtue looked up as Nash entered, with the whore, Angel, behind him.

"Good," he said to her, "you came."

She looked around.

"You are the sheriff now?" she asked.

"Sort of," he said. "He's letting me use his office." He looked at Nash. "Okay, Steve, you can go now."

"Sure."

Angel was dressed the way he wanted her to be, in a skirt and a peasant blouse. As Nash left, Virtue came around the desk, approached her and pulled the blouse down so that her big breasts bounced free.

"*Aye*," she said, "you are impatient."

He grabbed her breasts in his hands, squeezed them, pinched the nipples and then lifted them to his mouth so he could suck them first, then bite them. Her nipples were like grapes in his mouth.

"Are we not going to your hotel room?" she asked.

"Later, *chica*," he said, huskily, "much later. I need you right now and right here."

He backed away from her and said, "Strip. I want to watch."

147

She laughed, removed the blouse and her skirt and tossed them away. Then she stood and posed for him, her hands over her head, one knee slightly bent. He figured in ten years she'd be a fat pig, but right now she was just what he wanted, a whole lot of woman.

"Now undress me," he said. . . .

Charlie didn't have much else to prepare, so he went again with his meat and bean concoction, leaving out the eggs this time. When it was ready, he walked down the hall to Clint's room, found him lying on his side and sleeping soundly. He decided to eat without Clint and let him sleep. A while longer.

When she had him completely naked, she fell to her knees in front of him and took his rigid penis between her pillowy breasts. She rolled it there, pausing occasionally to reach down with her tongue and lick the tip. Finally, she swooped down on him with her hot mouth and took him completely inside. He moaned and reached for her head, held it gently first as she rode him wetly, then more forcefully, as if he thought she would stop. But Angel had no intention of stopping, and she suckled him until he roared and exploded into her mouth. . . .

Later, Virtue pinned her to the wall and entered her wet pussy from behind. He pounded her into the wall roughly, but she never complained. Angel liked it rough, which was why she was in demand as a whore. Most of the cowboys who came into town were rough because they didn't know any better. Not Virtue. He knew what he was doing, and she liked that.

Charlie took his plate and a beer to the bar. He stood so he could see outside, but no one outside could see him. The man Virtue had left across the street was leaning against a post, looking bored. He figured that man out back was probably even more bored. He might have worried they'd get so bored they'd try to break in, if Virtue hadn't explained that none of his men thought for themselves—ever.

Charlie decided that once this was over—and they came out of it alive—he was going to let Clint Adams off the hook. He was actually looking forward to riding through Mexico alone. And he wasn't feeling as depressed as he had been for years. Riding with Clint, having to take care of him a little bit, had done wonders for him. He was ready to go back out on his own again.

When he finished eating, he remembered the horses. He went to the storeroom and actually found a burlap sack filled with oats. Why Jerry Dunworthy had oats on hand he didn't know, but the horses were going to benefit from it.

Idly, as he fed the horses, he wondered if Dunworthy and his wife had actually fled town, and if so, did they even know that their daughter was dead, and that he had killed her?

And he wondered why he didn't feel worse about it.

They were in one of the jail cells, and Virtue now had Angel pinned beneath him on the cot. As he fucked her brutally, she turned her head and looked at the cell bars. She'd never been in jail before. Somehow the bars were adding to the experience for her.

Abruptly, Virtue stood up, taking her with him, then he turned and pinned her to the bars. The metal felt cold on her back, and one bar slid along the crack of her ass as he continued to have her.

She lifted her knees so she could wrap her legs around him. He was grunting with the effort of fucking her, and she knew she was going to have bruises in places she'd never had them before.

Virtue could feel the strain in his legs as he held her up against the bars. They were both sweating, and the small

cell was filled with the scent of sweat and sex. Finally,
when he couldn't hold her anymore, he grabbed her, turned
and backed up to the cot. This time when they fell on it, he
was on the bottom. She took control at that point, rode him
up and down, digging her nails into his chest, squeezing his
penis inside of her with muscles that had become trained
for just that task over the years. She squeezed him, milked
him, until he couldn't take it anymore. With another loud
bellow—he was also the loudest man she'd ever been
with—he exploded inside of her. . . .

THIRTY-SIX

Clint woke ravenous so Charlie brought a plate to him in his room, along with a beer.

"This is almost like havin' my own place again," he said.

"With horses in the rooms?" Clint asked.

"Well, that's a little different," Charlie admitted. "I found somethin' to feed them while you were asleep, so they're taken care of."

"That's good," Clint said. "What about our watchdogs?"

"Still there," Charlie said. "I don't know if they're the same ones, but they're there."

With a mouthful of meat and beans, Clint said, "I got an idea while I was asleep."

"You mean, like in a dream?"

"I guess I woke up with the idea," Clint said. "Don't know if it was a dream or not."

"Well, however you got it," Charlie said, "let's hear it."

Clint told him. It didn't take long. It was a pretty simple idea, and when he was done Charlie looked happy.

"I like it. How do we do it?"

"All I have to do," Clint said, "is stay on my feet long enough."

•   •   •

In the back of the building Pitt was wondering when he was going to get some relief. He was getting tired and hungry, and Nash had told him about this whorehouse in town he wanted to try. He was fidgeting from foot to foot, then stopped abruptly when the back door of the hotel opened. He started to reach for his gun, but nobody came out. The door had just swung open and there was nobody there.

He wondered what to do. All Virtue had told them was to watch, but this wasn't something expected. The hotel was supposed to be locked down tight. What was this door doing swinging open like that?

He stared at it for a while, wondering what to do.

Inside the building Charlie whispered to Clint, "If Virtue was right about his men and they really can't make their own minds up, this ain't gonna work. He'll stay out there all night and just watch."

"Well," Clint said, "if that's the case, one of us is just going to have to go out there and get him."

"Oh," Charlie said, "and I wonder which one of us that's gonna be?"

"That's easy," Clint said, "me."

Out front Thorpe was suffering the same pangs that Pitt was—hunger, for food and for a woman. And he was getting tired. Pretty soon he'd be too tired to go to a whorehouse. He'd be able to have one beer and then fall into bed for the night.

He was slouching, but stood straight up when he saw a light in the window across the street. It had only been dark about an hour, but he'd expected it to stay dark in the cantina. Why was there a light on? Just to rub it in that he was out here while they were in there, with food and whiskey and beer? And who knew, maybe they had women in there.

He wondered what Pitt was doing right about now.

• • •

Clint stepped out the back door, his stomach clenched. He didn't think the man would fire first, but you never knew. He kept his left hand against the wall of the hotel, and his right hand free. He didn't have his gunbelt on, because he still couldn't wear it. His Colt was stuck in his belt, but behind him. He wanted it to look as if he were unarmed.

Who could resist moving on an unarmed Gunsmith?

Pitt knew this was the Gunsmith, both from the description he'd been given and by the fact that the man was limping, obviously wounded.

And he looked unarmed.

Pitt couldn't resist. Maybe it was the hunger, or the sight of the great Gunsmith with no gun. He stepped out of the shadows, fronted Clint Adams and said, "Surprise."

Clint turned, looked at the man and said, "That's what I was going to say."

"What—"

"Just stand fast, mister," Charlie said from the hallway. "I got a rifle trained on your left ear."

Pitt froze. In that moment Clint pulled the gun from his belt and stuck it in Pit's face.

"Shit," Pitt said.

Thorpe couldn't believe his eyes. Was that Pitt standing in the window, waving at him? Waving *to* him? Telling him to come on? He was waving with his left hand, and in his right was his gun. How the hell did Pitt get the drop on both men?

However he did it, this meant that keeping watch was over. He could get some food, and maybe some pussy.

He stepped into the street and crossed over, light flooding out as the front door opened.

"Come on in, Harry," Pitt said.

THIRTY-SEVEN

Thorpe and Pitt glared at Charlie and Clint. It was all they could do, trussed up the way they were. Tied and gagged, disarmed and tossed into one of the rooms, all they had was a glare.

"That cuts down the odds a bit," Charlie said.

"Yeah," Clint said, "five to two isn't so bad."

"What do ya think Virtue will do when he realizes two of his men are gone?"

"I think he'll check the saloons and whorehouse before he decides maybe we got them. That should keep him busy for a little while."

"We're still gonna have to stand watch," Charlie said.

"Or sit," Clint said, "in my case."

"You up to it?"

"I had a nap," Clint said. "I can handle first watch."

"Maybe I'll just make double sure these fellas are tied nice and tight," Charlie said.

"I'm going to check on the horses," Clint said. "I haven't seen Eclipse since you brought him in."

Clint left the room and, while Charlie checked the ropes on Pitt and Thorpe, Clint went and looked in on Eclipse.

• • •

"I call," Horrigan said.

"I raise," Neal Jones said.

They were in the cantina, seated around a table with Mark Connors and Steve Nash.

"Del still got that whore in the jailhouse?" Connors asked.

"Far as I know," Nash said. "I'll call the raise."

"Me, too."

"Jesus," Jones said, "don't any of you scare out of a hand?"

"Not the way you bluff," Horrigan said. "I call the raise, too. Whataya got, Jones?"

"A full house," the man said, spreading his cards happily. "Kings over treys."

"Son of a bitch!" Horrigan snapped.

"Guess he wasn't bluffin' that time, Ben," Steve Nash said, tossing his cards in.

"Nice hand, Neal," Connors said, doing the same.

As Jones was raking in his money, Nash said, "Hey, ain't someone supposed to be relieving Thorpe and Pitt?"

"Yeah," Connors said, "but who?"

"I only got one thing to say," Horrigan commented. "Jones ain't leavin'. He's got too much of my money."

"There oughtta be a way we can decide who goes and who stays," Nash said.

"Yeah, there is," Jones said.

"What?"

"We can go and ask Del."

"I ain't botherin' him while he's with his whore," Connors said. "One of you can do it."

"I tell you what," Jones said. "Let's okay a few more hands before we decide."

"Why not?" Horrigan said. "Those boys are new, anyway. Won't hurt them to stand watch a while longer."

"Then deal the cards," Horrigan said to Connors.

• • •

Clint rubbed Eclipse on the nose and spoke to him gently.

"I know this isn't where you usually spend your nights, big boy," he said. "The same goes for me, too. Guess we'll both have to put up with it a while longer."

"You think he understands you?" Charlie asked, from the doorway.

"We understand each other," Clint said.

"I don't get it," Charlie said. "That mare and me, we don't communicate at all."

"Maybe you haven't been riding her long enough."

"It won't matter," Charlie said. "I just never got into the habit of talkin' ta horses."

Clint patted Eclipse's neck a few more times, then turned to leave the room. He and Charlie started down the hall.

"How you doin'?" Charlie asked.

"Better."

"Strength in that leg?"

"Yeah," Clint lied.

"Then yer limpin' for no good reason?"

"I'm limping because I got shot, Charlie," Clint said, "but it's feelin' a lot better."

"I'll get you set up in the hall," Charlie said.

"We better get up early in the morning," Clint said. "We don't know what time Virtue will make his move."

"Like you said," Charlie replied, putting a couple of pillows in a chair in the hall for him, "he may spend some time tryin' to find these two."

"Give us time to have breakfast before we have to go out and face them," Clint said.

"That it?" Charlies asked. "We just gonna walk out the front door and do it?"

"Unless I can dream up a better idea," Clint said. "Or you can."

"Can't say as I ever got an idea in a dream before," Charlie said, "but then most of my dreams have been nightmares for a long time."

"I'm confident," Clint said, settling into his chair, "that by morning one of us will have a brilliant idea."

"Well," Charlie said, "I just hope you're confident enough for the both of us."

THIRTY-EIGHT

It was a couple of hours before the poker players finally decided that Ben Horrigan and Mark Connors should go and relieve Thorpe and Pitt.

"Send them back here," Nash said, "and tell them to bring money."

When no one returned in a half hour, Nash said to Neal Jones, "What the hell is holdin' them up?"

"You in a hurry because I'm beatin' you head-to-head?"

"Just deal the cards," Nash said. "We'll see who beats who."

After an hour both Horrigan and Connors came back in, looking both puzzled and worried.

"What the hell—" Nash said.

"I thought you were relieving them other two," Jones said.

"They ain't there," Horrigan said.

"What?" Nash asked.

"We looked all over for 'em," Connors said. "We can't find 'em."

"Well, what the hell happened to them?" Nash asked. "They can't just vanish."

"Maybe they took off," Connors said. "Didn't like the deal and left."

"Naw, Thorpe wouldn't do that," Nash said.

"Maybe they went to the whorehouse," Jones suggested.

"Thorpe would do that," Nash said, "but they'd go one at a time. Did you look around behind the hotel?"

"Behind and on both sides," Horrigan said. "Nothin'."

There was a long moment of silence, then Connors asked, "So what do we do?" followed by another long moment of silence. None of them was used to making decisions.

Finally Horrigan said, "I say we don't do nothin'."

"You don't think we should tell Del?" Jones asked.

"Hell, no," Horrigan said. "He'll wanna know why we were so late in lookin' for them. You wanna tell him we was busy playin' cards?"

"What about the whorehouse?" Nash asked. "We could look there."

"If they're at the whorehouse, let them explain that to Del tomorrow," Horrigan said. "I'm gonna go stand watch like I'm supposed to."

"Me, too," Connors said.

"When Del asks, we'll just say they wasn't there when we went to relieve them," Horrigan said. "Let them fend for themselves. Agreed?"

Everybody nodded.

"We got to stay together on this," Horrigan warned.

"Okay," Nash said. "We'll all tell the same story."

Horrigan nodded and he and Connors went back to the hotel.

"Deal 'em out," Nash said to Jones. "My luck's about to change."

"I am bruised everywhere," Angel said, "but I must go back to work."

Virtue was lying on a cot in one of the cells, still naked.

He was watching her get dressed, her big breasts and buttocks disappearing into her clothes.

"Stay here the whole night," he said.

"You are mad," she said. "That would kill me . . . or
you . . . or both of us. Besides, aren't you afraid *el jefe* will
come back?"

"I tol' you, he ain't comin' back," Virtue said, "and neither are any of his deputy *jefes*. This place is mine, now."

Angel gave Virtue a worried look.

"You did not kill him, did you?"

"No, of course I didn't kill him," Virtue said. "He just
sort of . . . resigned."

"Resigned?"

"Quit."

"Ah," she said, "*reuncie. Deje.*"

"Right," he said, unsure of what she was saying, "quit."

"And you wish me to stay all night?" she asked.

"Yes."

"And sleep in a cell?"

"Sure, why not?"

Oddly, the thought thrilled her. She had never spent the
night in a jail cell before.

"I still have to go back and tell them," she said.

"Of course."

"And you will pay?"

"Yes."

"All right," she said, with a smile, "yes, I will stay with
you the night here, in the jail."

"Good." He got up and pulled on his pants. "I'll make
some coffee. It'll be ready when you get back."

"Coffee?"

"Yes," he replied, "we can sit and talk and have coffee
when you come back."

"And then we fuck some more?" she asked.

"Hell, yeah," he said, "and then we fuck some more."

"But then we sleep, eh?"

"Okay," he said, "we can sleep, too."

She suddenly seemed struck by a wonderful idea.

"And I will bring back some food, eh?"

"Good," he said, "that sounds great. Bring back some food. We'll eat, we'll drink, we'll sleep . . ."

". . . and we fuck."

"Oh yeah," he said, liking her more and more, "and then we will definitely fuck."

THIRTY-NINE

When Clint decided to stretch his legs—and his hip—he walked to the front of the cantina, did not light any lamps and peered out the front window. Sure enough, he saw a man standing across the street. Had they replaced the watchers without wondering where the original two went?

He walked to one of the back rooms and did the same, left it dark and looked out the window. It took a moment, but he finally saw someone in the shadows.

He went back to his chair in the hall and sat down. Virtue was either unfazed by the fact that two of his men had disappeared, or he didn't know yet. Maybe the other men were looking for them, covering for them, or simply throwing them to the dogs. Maybe they found the two men missing and, as Virtue himself had said, could not decide what to do, so they simply replaced them. In the morning, when Virtue found out what had happened, he'd be the one making the decisions.

Five-to-two odds should still suit Del Virtue, especially with Clint Adams wounded. He might spend some time looking for the missing men, but in the end he'd go ahead and make his play.

Clint hoped his leg and hip would stand up to the pressure just long enough. He wasn't going to be able to make any quick move, like ducking for cover, so every shot he made was going to have to count. He just hoped that every shot Charlie made counted, as well.

When Charlie woke Clint the next morning, he said, "Same old stuff for dinner."

"Still better than cold beans on the trail," Clint said. "See our new friends?" He'd told Charlie about them when he woke him for his watch.

"Yep, they're still there. Whataya think happened?"

"I was wondering," Clint said, sitting up and putting his feet on the floor. "They're probably waiting for the boss to decide what to do."

"Well, I checked our friends. They're still tied up nice and tight. They were even snorin', sleepin' like babies."

"I guess we ought to feed them."

"I made extra," Charlie said, "even though I'm tempted not to feed them. What's the difference? If we end up dead, they'll be cut loose. And if we end up still standin', they'll be cut loose."

"You're right," Clint said. "To hell with them. Let them go hungry for a while."

"Well, come on," Charlie said. "We might as well eat. If we're gonna die today, it might as well be on a full stomach."

Clint agreed. He limped after Charlie to the kitchen, but by the time they got there his leg had already stretched out and felt stronger.

Virtue woke in the cell with Angel lying on top of him on the cot. It had been the wildest night he'd ever spent in a jail cell and, like her, he had bruises in places he'd never had bruises before. If he'd had to sit a horse today, he didn't know if he would have been able to do it.

He slapped Angel on her big ass to wake her up.

"*Aye!*" she said. "Not again."

"No," he said, "not again. It's mornin' and I have to get up."

She frowned, then rolled off him, almost falling off the cot. She got to her feet and, totally naked, stretched.

"You keep doin' that and I am gonna wanna go again," he said. "Put on some clothes, woman."

She smiled at him as she slipped her blouse on over her head and pulled on her skirt. At the same time he grabbed his shirt and pants, then sat on the cot to pull on his boots.

"I have to go home to bed," she said.

"Go ahead."

"You have to pay me."

"Pay you?" he asked.

"*Sí*," she said, "you tol' me you would pay for the whole night."

"I'll have to pay you later," he said, "after I go to the bank."

"The bank?"

"That's where they have money."

"*Sí*, I know what a bank is," she said. "You do not live in town, so you do not have an account at the bank."

"I, uh, have to collect a reward," he lied.

"A reward."

"A bounty?"

She frowned. "I do not believe you."

"Okay," he said, standing up, "you got me. I ain't gonna pay you."

"But . . . we spent the night together."

"And it was great," he said. "Here." He handed her ten dollars.

"Ten dollars? You owe me more than ten dollars."

"Angel," he said, slowly, "why don't you leave before I take back the ten dollars."

"*Cabrone*," she cursed. "You will pay me." Her black eyes were flashing. "Or else."

His hand flashed out suddenly and he grabbed her by the throat. Her eyes bulged and her nostrils flared.

"Look," he said, "you are a great piece of ass, Angel, but I don't intend to pay you, and I'll be leavin' town soon. I just have one little thing to attend to this mornin'." He put his face close to hers. "I have to kill two men."

Her bulging eyes widened even more.

"Do you want me to add you to my list?"

She shook her head.

"Good," he said, "we understand each other, right?"

She nodded.

He released his hold on her neck and said, "Get out."

She turned and ran out, passing Steve Nash, who was on the way in. Virtue came out of the cell block and saw Nash. There was something in his face he didn't like.

"What happened now?" he asked.

FORTY

Clint and Charlie brought their weapons out to the cantina and sat at a table checking them, cleaning them, making sure they were in proper working order.

"How do we do this?" Charlie asked. "Bill always told me who he'd handle, who I should handle . . . it always worked real well for us."

Clint thought a moment.

"I'm guessing since there's five of them left that Virtue will be in the center," Clint said. "The others will take their cue from him. We'll deal with them right to left, okay?"

"Sure."

"I'll take Virtue and the two to our left," Clint said, "you take the two to our right."

"Okay."

"What do you handle better, Charlie, a handgun or a rifle?"

"Usually, a rifle."

"I've got an idea. Get that Greener from behind the bar."

Charlie went to the bar, reached over, found the shotgun and brought it back to the table.

"Give it here,"

Clint took the Greener, broke it open, unloaded it, then checked it.

"Aside from being dirty, it looks fine," he said. "I think you should carry this."

"And my rifle?"

"No, this and your handgun. Fire these barrels one at a time, then drop it and draw your gun. You may not need your pistol after this, but have it out, anyway."

"Gotcha."

Clint happened to know that a shotgun worked very well for Doc Holliday in Tombstone when he was backing the play of the Earps against the Clanton gang. He'd also seen it work well himself.

"I'll clean it and reload it," Clint said. "Why don't you check out front? We don't know how much warning we're going to have."

While Clint worked on the shotgun, Charlie went to the front window and looked out.

"Just one man, so far," he said.

"Good, then we've got time."

Charlie went back to the table and worked on his own pistol. Eventually, Clint reloaded the shotgun and snapped it shut.

"Won't know how well it works until we try it," he told Charlie, handing it back.

Charlie looked down at it, then looked at Clint and said, "I don't find that too encouraging."

"It'll work," Clint said. "I guarantee it."

"Okay."

Clint hesitated, then added, "Just remember not to pull both triggers at the same time."

Charlie stared at Clint.

"Well, the barrel might . . . explode."

"Wha—"

"I'm just kidding."

•   •   •

Del Virtue sat in the sheriff's office, fuming. He had Nash and Jones out scouring the town for Thorpe and Pitt. He didn't know who he was more mad at, them or Nash for suggesting them.

Without those two the odds were down to five-to-two, worse than they were in Magdalena. Not that it mattered. He still felt they were more than capable of killing the Gunsmith and his friend. But he wasn't about to let Thorpe and Pitt off easy, especially since they had just joined the gang.

They weren't going to last very long. . . .

Nash and Jones came back to the jailhouse at the same time.

"Well?" Virtue asked.

"No sign of them anywhere," Nash said.

"Not even at the whorehouse," Jones said.

Virtue stared at them.

"Okay," he said, "there's only one other explanation."

"What's that, Del?" Nash asked.

"Adams got them."

"What?" Jones asked. "How?"

"I don't know how, but he did," Virtue said. "He's got them inside that building."

"What are we gonna do, then?" Nash asked. "Get them out?"

"Nothin'," Virtue said, "at least, nothin' about them. What we're gonna do is what we came here to do."

"The five of us?" Nash asked.

"Yes," Virtue said, "the five of us."

Nash and Jones exchanged a glance, then shrugged as Virtue stood up.

"When do we do it, Del?" Nash asked.

"Now," Del Virtue said, "we're gonna go and do it right now. Ben and Mark over there?"

"They should be," Nash said, "unless they're missin', too."

"Let's go and find out."

FORTY-ONE

Clint suggested they both just sit in the cantina and wait.

"Shouldn't one of us watch the back?" Charlie asked.

"When they come, they'll come to the front."

"What about still tryin' ta ride out?"

"They'll come after us, Charlie," Clint said. "We've got to finish it here and now."

So they sat, away from the window but in position to see out the front. When Virtue and his men began to gather out there, they saw them.

"Looks like four," Charlie said, then, "wait, looks like they're sendin' one to the back to get the fifth man." He looked at Clint. "I could run back there and try to pick them off."

"We've already discussed it too long," Clint said. "You'd probably be too late."

While they watched, the fourth man reappeared with the fifth in tow. All five men then removed their handguns and checked them, then slid them back into their holsters.

"Here they come . . ." Clint said.

Virtue stepped into the street first, followed by his men, two to his right and two to his left.

"We're gonna get this done today," he'd told them. "Any argument?" He was looking right at Ben Horrigan.

"What're ya lookin' at me for?" Horrigan complained. "I been ready for weeks."

"You're the one always has somethin' to say, Ben," Virtue pointed out.

"Well, not today," Horrigan responded. "Today I'm just ready to get it over with and get on with my life."

"Then let's do it," Virtue said and started across the street.

"Jesus," Charlie said, as the men approached, "they're comin' just like you said they would, two to his right, two to his left."

"Men like Del Virtue usually don't have much of an imagination, Charlie," Clint explained.

"Adams!" Virtue's voiced called. "Clint Adams. I'm callin' you out!"

"See what I mean?" Clint asked.

Virtue stopped in the center of the street. Word had obviously already spread that there was something brewing. The street was empty, and there were eyes peering around curtains and out windows along the street. With no law in town, the people just had to wait for the scene to play itself out.

"Adams!" Virtue shouted. "Clint Adams! This is Del Virtue. I said I'm calling you and Charlie Utter out."

Virtue could feel his men fidgeting on either side of him. They were anxious, but they were good men. He was confident.

Charlie turned from the window and looked over at Clint, who stood up and walked over to stand by him.

"You ready?" Clint asked.

"As I'll ever be," Charlie said, hefting the shotgun.

Del Virtue called his name one more time. Clint cracked

the door open. There were no batwings on the cantina doorway.

"I hear you, Virtue."

"Are you comin' out?" Virtue shouted. "Or are we comin' in?"

"If we don't come out, I doubt you can come in," Clint said. "Not all of you, anyway."

"Maybe you wanna try runnin' out the back again?"

"No," Clint said, "I'm pretty much committed to getting this over and done, this time. That is, unless you and your boys have had a change of heart?"

"Not after ridin' all this way, we ain't," Virtue said. "Say, you got my other two men in there?"

"They're here," Clint said. "They were a little too curious last night. They're out of the play until it's all over."

"That's okay," Virtue said. "My original four and me are plenty."

"Well," Clint said, "you're about to get your wish. We're coming out."

"Come ahead," Virtue said. "We'll let you get set."

Clint turned to Charlie.

"They're more liable to start firing as soon as we're out there. So be ready."

"I'm ready."

"And don't mind me," Clint said. "You hit the ground if you have to. I'll most likely use a post to hold myself up."

"Might be safer if you just fell down," Charlie said.

"You're probably right about that."

Clint grabbed the door, took a deep breath and swung it wide open. There were no shots. Looked like they were going to let Clint and Charlie both step out before they started shooting.

"Let's go," he said to Charlie.

As the door opened, Virtue said to his men, "Don't let them get set. As soon as they're both out, we start shootin'."

FORTY-TWO

Clint stepped out onto the boardwalk first, reached out with his left hand for one of the posts. Charlie came out behind him, holding the shotgun ready. True enough, as soon as Virtue and his men were able to see both of them, they drew and fired.

The first shot struck the post near Clint's hand. Almost immediately Charlie let go with one barrel, then threw himself into a roll as a volley of shots hit the door behind him.

Clint drew and fired, but his hip twinged at that moment. His shot, meant for the center of Virtue's torso, hit the man in the left arm. Virtue immediately went into a crouch.

Clint fired again, this time taking the man to Virtue's right in the belly. Ben Horrigan doubled over, screamed and then fell silent.

Charlie's first barrel had been fired in haste, and most of the shot hit the ground. A few pellets struck Steve Nash in the chest, but while they were painful, they weren't fatal.

Charlie came out of his roll on one knee, turned the shotgun and pulled the second trigger. This time he was more accurate. Most of the shot hit Neal Jones right in the

175

abdomen, killing him instantly, leaving him a riddled mess on the street.

That left Virtue on one knee, Nash and Mark Connors still standing and firing.

One bullet struck Charlie's cheek with a glancing blow, another hit him in the left arm. He cried out, dropped the shotgun into the street and drew his pistol.

Clint fired again, this time hitting Mark Connors square in the chest, knocking him back and then down.

Charlie fired three times at Steve Nash, hitting him once. The bullet struck him in the throat, immediately filling his mouth with blood. He started to strangle on it, but died before that could happen.

Clint released his hold on the post and stepped down into the street. But his leg gave out and he went sprawling into the street, holding tightly to his gun.

Virtue had fired a split second before that. If Clint had not fallen, the bullet would have hit him in the chest. From a prone position he snapped one shot off at Virtue, hitting him in the hip. At that moment Charlie fired two more times, and one of his bullets hit Del Virtue in the chest. There was gun smoke and dust all around and Clint had trouble seeing the men in the street, but it had suddenly gone quiet.

"Charlie, stay where you are," Clint called out. "Let the smoke clear."

They waited. The dust settled down and the smoke drifted up, revealing a sad picture. All five men were sprawled in the street, bloody and dead.

"Clint?"

"I'm okay. You?"

"I'll live."

"Check them out, Charlie," Clint said, "Make sure they're all dead."

"Gotcha."

Charlie rushed forward, and as he approached each man

he kicked their guns away from them. As people came out to see the aftermath of the gun battle, Charlie bent over each man.

"They're dead, Clint."

Clint got painfully to one knee, half crawled over to a hitching post and used it to get to his feet. Hastily, he ejected the empty shells from his gun and reloaded, just in case.

Charlie came over and stood by him. Clint noticed the blood on the man's cheek and his arm.

"How bad?" he asked.

"Creased both times," Charlie said. "I ain't carryin' nobody's lead."

"That's good."

People began to mill around, men, women and some children, a few stepping into the street to take a look.

"Take out that badge and put it on," Clint said.

"But I ain't the sheriff."

"These people will respond to the tin," Clint said. "Get them to clear the street and get some men to clear away the bodies."

"And after that?"

"After that, I guess we'll have to leave them to themselves. They'll have to figure out on their own who their new lawman is."

"And the two inside?"

"We'll let them go," Clint said. "I don't think they'll be any trouble. Not after they see what happened here."

"What are you gonna do?" Charlie asked.

Clint sat down on the boardwalk right in front of the cantina.

"I'm going to sit here and catch my breath."

FORTY-THREE

Clint was sitting in a chair outside the cantina, playing back the scene that had occurred on the street right out front a little more than a week ago. All the blood was gone, having long since soaked into the dirt, but in his head he could still see the dead bodies strewn about. They had released Thorpe and Pitt while the bodies were still there, and both men had immediately collected their horses and ridden out of town.

In the aftermath of the killings a new sheriff had been appointed. Clint was of the opinion that the man was secretly grateful that he hadn't been sheriff until after the event. Also, they had decided to remain in the cantina until Clint was ready to ride. Jerry and his whore wife, Theresa, had never returned, so the ownership of the building was up in the air.

But today was the day they were leaving. They had returned the horses to the livery the morning of the shooting. Better to get rid of the smell if they were going to continue to stay there. Now Charlie had gone to get them, and Clint saw him walking up the street leading both animals. People were watching him, but no one was catching his eye.

When he reached the cantina, he tied both horses to a post and stepped up onto the boardwalk.

"Are you sure you wanna do this, Clint?" he asked. "You know, the doc says you still need a week, maybe two."

"I'm ready," Clint said. "I'll take a leisurely ride to Labyrinth, Texas, and get some rest there. My invitation is still open, you know."

"I appreciate it," Charlie said, "but I'm still set on seein' ol' Mexico, and this close I can't see changin' my mind."

"I don't blame you."

The doc had patched up Charlie's wounds, but they had faded pretty quickly. There was just the hint of a scar on his cheek, smaller than Clint's permanent one.

"We had a helluva time here, huh?" Charlie asked.

"Yeah, we did, Charlie," Clint said, "and if you don't mind, I'm not real anxious to ever repeat it."

"Yeah, me neither," Charlie said, although Clint didn't believe him. He thought the whole experience had taken Charlie back a dozen years to his life with Bill Hickok.

"Well," Clint said, "time to go."

He got up from the chair, careful not to let Charlie see him wince. He knew he was taking a chance riding so soon, but he had a hankering to get out of El Paso that just wouldn't quit.

"Bet the folks here can't see us leave too soon," Charlie said, as they stepped down from the boardwalk and approached their horses.

"We livened the place up some, that's for sure," Clint said. "Might calm down a bit after we leave, but that won't last. Border towns like this don't stay calm for long."

Clint waited until Charlie was in the act of mounting, and then dragged himself up onto Eclipse's back. It took too long and he found Charlie watching him by the time he was upright.

"What?" he asked. "I'll be fine."

"Maybe I should ride to Labyrinth with you, just to keep you from falling off your animal."

"If you want to come with me that's fine, but not to keep me from falling off," Clint said. "I don't want to keep you from Mexico."

"I could always cross into Mexico later—"

"Like you said, this close you'd be foolish not to go," Clint said. "Coming with me will only take you farther away."

"Yeah, you're right," Charlie said. "Besides, if you do fall off it'll be your own damn fault."

"You got that right."

The two men had to go in different directions right from there, so Charlie extended his hand.

"Appreciate everythin', Clint."

"You kept me alive, Charlie," Clint said.

"Maybe, but you brought me back to life. Can't thank ya enough for that."

"We'll cross paths again, Charlie."

"Maybe," Charlie said. "You never know. I just may like it so much in Mexico I'll never come back."

"There's worse places to live."

AUTHOR'S NOTE

It's a fact that after Deadwood and the death of Wild Bill Hickok, Charlie Utter wandered from place to place. As late as 1881 he was actually running a saloon in Socorro, New Mexico. After that, though, history completely loses track of Charlie Utter. So who's to say he didn't go down to ol' Mexico and just start over?

Watch for

TWO FOR TROUBLE

303rd novel in the exciting GUNSMITH series
from Jove

Coming in March!

GIANT ACTION! GIANT ADVENTURE!

THE GUNSMITH

GIANT

Giant Westerns featuring The Gunsmith

LITTLE SURESHOT AND THE WILD WEST SHOW
0-515-13851-7

DEAD WEIGHT
0-515-14028-7

RED MOUNTAIN
0-515-14206-9

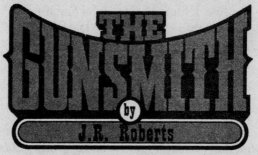